So anyway...

a collection of
short stories

*To David
With very best
wishes from*

Vic

Vic Blake

So anyway...
Vic Blake

www.vicblakewriter.co.uk

The right of the author to be identified as the author of this work
has been asserted in accordance with the
Copyright, Designs and Patents Act 1988.

ISBN 978-1-910779-81-1 (Paperback)

Typeset by
Oxford eBooks Ltd.
www.oxford-ebooks.com

*It is my absolute pleasure to dedicate this
volume with all my love and best wishes to
Maggie, my ever-patient wife, and to my two sons
and four grandchildren, all of whom I love beyond
mere words.*

Acknowledgements

First of all I should like to extend my sincere thanks and gratitude to the all the members of the Mapperley and District U3A Creative Writing Group, past and present, who provided me with both the inspiration and the impetus for putting so much of this collection together. Thank you all for your patience, your undivided attention and your constructive support while I tried out these stories on you in their formative stages.

I also wish to thank all my dear friends and colleagues in the East Midlands Ageing Men's Group for their invaluable support, encouragement and constant friendship over so many years, as well as for their regular comments on these stories.

Thank you, too, Richard Johnson for so painstakingly going through the early draft, for your always constructive comments, and for all the work you put into the foreword for this volume.

A special thank you, as well, to Andy Severn of Oxford eBooks for all your work and expertise in preparing this for publication. This probably would not have happened without you.

Last, but far from least, I really want to thank Maggie, my wife, my dearest friend and fellow traveller for so many years for your love, for your support, your endless patience and your inspiration. I truly am a very Lucky Man – and I do recognise my good luck when I see it!

Foreword

Richard Johnson

I must have known Vic for almost 20 years since we met in our Ageing Men's Group, of which we were both early members. Vic came to this group from the practice of psychotherapeutic counselling and a pro-feminist form of men's politics, myself from teaching cultural studies at Birmingham and Nottingham Trent universities. As time went on, we worked together on a collective project in men's memory work and met outside the group to share our current projects in philosophy, theories of identity and education, Vic with a psycho-social slant, myself with a renewed interest in history.

As a sole author, I first read Vic as an analyst of gender relations and of masculinity in particular, then as a gifted poet. Although we had been telling each other stories for a long time, his short stories were new to me and, it seems to him, a discovery of a new and creative third age. When he asked me to consider writing this foreword, it seemed an enormous responsibility but also, I must say, increasingly a pleasure.

There seemed to me to be a marked development of mastery of the short-story form as this collection progressed, so it is interesting to read that they are presented more or less in the order in which they were written. There are some telling stories in the first 30 pages or so: *The Waiting Room* anticipates many features of the later stories; the *Unlucky Man* explores in a unique and intriguing form, borrowed from folklore, the ethics of responsibility and fault, of faithlessness and providential justice. Other early stories depend on sympathy for a main character up against the odds in different ways, or the intrigue of a mysterious woman or of a magical trick.

My favourite stories, however, come thick and fast in the second part of the collection, roughly from *Love For Beginners* and *Beeswing*. Many of these later stories exploit a similar narrative strategy. First we are introduced to a character or characters through ordinary everyday homely doings that tend to produce a feeling of comfortable familiarity: enjoying the company of dog and neighbours; waking up cosily in bed, planning a perfect day; enjoying new-found skills or a new relationship, or just coping with the details of a demanding life.

Then, there may emerge a slower strangeness in the story, or a more sudden shift of mood, a revelation that makes you read back for clues, or a shock or a twist that destroys the comfort, disrupts the expectations. In some stories 'destroys' is perhaps too harsh a word, for the turnabout may be wrapped in humour, though it may still unease. But each time we are drawn, often with pleasure, into the story: a happy Christmas; a gossipy coffee morning; a satisfying piece of manual labour; a sexually inviting encounter; a chance for love - until a disaster happens, a threat looms, a secret is revealed (or not), and the whole collapses in helpless laughter or ends with a sinister grin.

What are these stories about then, explicitly or in their more covert ways? Perhaps I draw on 'external evidence' when I say that most of the stories, perhaps not all, are about gender. There is only one story – *Boys and Girls* – where the critical gender analyst is heard in his own voice, telling us explicitly the moral point of two related sets of happenings. Cumulatively, however, the stories produce an account of men and women, boys and girls, not entirely fixed in these categories, but playing them out in different ways.

There are marked sympathies or identifications with women and children in these 21 stories. Seven are vocalised through women; it is the woman's point of view which is prioritised in the narrative, while four stories employ a child's point of view, including one girl's.

Women are present and often predominant, even powerful in many of the stories, so there is no way that what is portrayed is 'a man's world'. There are one or two stories where women are victims of male brutality or control but more often it is the women that make things happen; certainly express love, caring and desire, but also exact revenge, leave a boring relationship for a more interesting life, challenge men, investigate mysteries, make magic, shape-shift in disturbing ways, and even commit murder. In other words, women are often powerful, at least in the small-scale domestic and relational sphere which is traditionally their own.

Boys and men are vulnerable beings, not at all in control, or only by convention, and in some tension with their natures. They are rendered distraught by paternal neglect or by the consequences of their own hyper risk-taking and competition. They are puzzled, verbally attacked and even killed or disappeared. Sometimes the aggressor – more often they – are the ones that seem to be in danger, even unto death.

There is however no simple inversion of gender power; it is as though the power ascribed to men simply does not work, either to accomplish their desires, or to achieve a prescribed identity. Masculinity, 'as we 'know it' – or are supposed to – seems impossible, or just too uncomfortable or perilous by half. Given the visibility of women's points of view, gender power seems to move fluidly and is two-way.

In hetero-sexual relations, boys and men do objectify women, but these conventions of male power are themselves seen as fragile, marking puzzlement and vulnerability much more than stereotypical machismo, adventure-story heroism or cool control. This is true even of the boy group cultures, portrayed here, classically a source of the policing of masculinities. Men may even desire to be more like women, at least in some particular respect. Even, in what is perhaps my favourite story, for its period feel, its capturing of working-class handiness and its delightful and apparently secure romance, a shadow falls on the young man's manhood.

I return to the characteristic combination in the form of these stories, or what to me are the best ones; so much kindly humour and sympathy and even comfort, caught through daily details, but also much unsettlement and thoughtful reflection on our contemporary gender troubles.

How good it is to find a male author confident and knowledgeable enough to write about the contradictions of living as a man!

Table of Contents

Introduction

The idea for this collection emerged out of my almost complete Covid lockdown during 2020/21. I had already started writing fiction, partly as a diversion from more academic writing, so I already had several short stories on file. But there is nothing like a long period of confinement to concentrate the mind in the direction of a 'project' of some kind. Thus a book – or at least the idea of a book – was born. What I needed to do now was to write some more and then to pull it all together into a Collection.

All these stories are short enough to be read over a cup of tea and touch upon a wide variety of themes ranging from love and love-gone-wrong, to why on earth do so many of our socks go missing in the wash!

Thematically, however, several of them focus in specifically on the gender of the character and, more notably, men and their inner lives as they struggle, in their various ways, with the trials of masculinity; with love, sex, and relationships more generally.

While these will inevitably draw upon my own experience and my time as a counsellor working with men, they also owe a debt of gratitude to the frank, sharing, and trusting relationships built up over many years with close friends in two local men's groups. I do hope as well, however, that my approach to this subject might make these stories that much more interesting and insightful for women readers too.

These are stories of a particular kind in that most were conceived in response to suggestions from my local U3A[1] Creative Writing Group and I owe them a debt of gratitude for their ideas and suggestions, and for their patience in listening so attentively while I read them my earlier drafts. On this point it is worth noting as well that all these stories were written specifically to be read out loud, and my sometimes quirky use of punctuation reflects this. For similar reasons, each story needed to be of economical length simply so that everyone in the group should get their chance to read out their own stories.

Two stories (*The Photograph* and *Boys and Girls*) are based on personal experience. In contrast, *The Unlucky Man*, is my version of a traditional story which I first heard when living in Galicia in the north west of Spain. *Spin Cycle*, on the other hand, had been churning away in my head for a long time.

Now, in my seventies, I am so happy that I never really lost my childhood free-flights of imagination and my choice of front cover is intended to reflect this. And while the hard realities of adulthood eventually loom ever-larger, being able now to channel this imagination into my writing has been an immense pleasure for me.

Lastly, there is no particular running order to these stories. They run, more-or-less, in the order in which they were written, with only a loose attempt to conserve the overall tone and contours of the volume.

So anyway… if you have picked up this volume, all I can say is that I hope you enjoy my efforts as much as I did. And thank you for doing so.

---

1   University of the Third Age

1

The Waiting Room

You could tell Jeanette McCredie was not well just by looking at her. Though she could hardly be described as old, her painful stoop, the dark-shadowed eyes, the deep-set lines in her face, all were signs that the years had not been especially kind to her. Bent against a bitter wind, she shuffled up to the big glass doors to the clinic and, being as her left arm was folded in a sling, she pushed hard against her own reflection with her right shoulder, grimacing painfully as she did so.

Once out of the wind she straightened up just a little. The waiting room was bright and airy and plenty warm enough and she drew a long breath and paused for a few moments before checking in at the reception desk.

The receptionist received and processed her as though she were on remote control: 'Name? Date of birth? Address? Doctor's name?'

Only then did she look up and, with just a tinge of kindness in her tone, invited her to take a seat.

'The Doctor will be with you shortly,' she added.

There were several empty chairs around the walls, although there was only one empty pair, so she chose the one next to the woman in the short skirt, rather than the young man with the shaved head, and eased herself into it with a feeling of blessed relief.

The clock on the wall opposite said that she had just short

of fifteen minutes to wait for her appointment. She checked it absent-mindedly against her watch, which was always wrong anyway, and then glanced about her. Beneath the clock there was a white-board on which someone had printed a message in blue felt tip pen indicating that appointments today were running about ten minutes late. She didn't choose a magazine to read but instead sat there, looking around the room, but at no-one in particular, and thought about her daughter.

Mairead was a beautiful young woman, intelligent and cheery and with a bright future ahead of her. She was married to John, a junior partner in a law firm, and they had a lovely daughter, Rosa, now aged nine. But Mairead had fizzy feet and had always found it difficult to remain in one place for very long. It was possible that her affair with James Leroux, an old college friend, may not have been her first but, once it came to light, her marriage became a war zone, and when John finally announced that he was leaving her and taking Rosa to England, Mairead crumbled. She became deeply depressed and unable to work and, although she sought help, it did her little good. Then, a year ago last April and without warning, she took her own beautiful life.

Jeanette sat and stared glassily into space, feeling very alone. Like the Troubles, the time for tears had almost gone and she had settled into a self-protective state of numb resignation with no interests and few friends to speak of. She hadn't seen or heard from Rosa since last summer and lately she had even stopped attending her church, leaving her even more isolated.

Suddenly the young man next to her broke into a bout of loud coughing and, with her trance broken, Jeanette became aware that he didn't actually smell very nice. She shuffled slightly closer to the woman on her left and looked up again at the clock. Still a while to go.

So she was taken aback slightly when, only a few moments

later, a rather overweight nurse appeared from a doorway and announced, with the voice of a bored teenager:

'Jeanette McCredie for Mr Leroux.'

Jeanette's heart thumped like a fist in her chest. She felt momentarily for her dead husband's pistol concealed in her sling and then painfully, but determinedly, eased herself to her feet.

2

Missing

The letter, all those years ago, had been quite brief but politely worded and thoughtful. The writer, probably some minor functionary or other in the public relations department, had apologised for the mistake – entirely inexplicable as it was – and had sent Abigail two new boxes of chocolates by way of compensation; one the same as the faulty box in question, the other a sumptuous, top-of-the-range luxury assortment.

The company were at a loss to explain how one chocolate came to be missing from the original sealed box and were at pains to stress that, with all the rigorous checks and balances they had in place, it really ought never to have happened. Still, they were good enough not to labour the point and seemed prepared to take Abigail at her word, with any reservations they may have harboured about her honesty being confined to a barely discernible point of emphasis near the end; that this was an 'act of goodwill' on their part.

Abigail was more than happy with the result. She read the letter several times, her eyes flitting back and forth from letter to chocolates and from chocolates to letter, not quite believing her good luck. She was so pleased with herself now for sending off her letter of complaint. It had taken her ages to compose and she nervously screwed up and discarded several attempts before she got it right. And then came the actual posting, that final moment of commitment after which the fates alone would determine the outcome.

Her equally pleased family got to finish off the original box with her and still had two more boxes to go. One of these they consumed, for a special treat, eking them out over the course of the following weekend, but the larger box, the luxury assortment, they kept back for Christmas, still six weeks away, when all the family could once again indulge themselves with glorious chocolate while revelling once again in their unexpected good fortune.

'Good old Mum!'

'Yay!'

After Christmas the remaining empty box went in the bin and the memory soon began to subside, though the stories were sometimes re-told along with ecstatic outpourings as to which were their personal favourites and how scrummy they were. Dad, with runny caramel drooling into his moustache and not realising until much later, was a favourite recollection of the children's. Abigail too dined out on the stories to friends and workmates and to great attention and acclaim.

'Ooooh! I'll have to try that', several of them said, laughing loudly and giving her a friendly 'only-kidding' shove on the shoulder.

But with time the stories, having completed their rounds, faded, surfacing again only rarely, such as when the company was fresh and when gaps in the conversation were looking to be filled. Twenty five years on, the incident was all but forgotten.

'Tony! Quick, he's on!' Abigail called to her husband who was in the kitchen pouring himself another glass of beer. He returned to find the television on 'pause' and Abigail perched on the edge of her seat, remote control at the ready and a glass of Sauvignon Blanc beside her on the coffee table. After three decades she was fuller of figure now and her hair was starting to turn grey at the edges, but she was still in good shape and still had that twinkle in her eye which flashed like a diamond when she was excited.

The television was un-paused and Marty McCoy burst loudly into life in his usual tuxedo and black bow tie. Abigail turned the volume down a little as they watched the near-manic host of the show prime his applauding audience like a class of infants:

'So… what did you think of that, Ladies and Gentlemen? *Very* good, wasn't he! How on Earth he did that thing with the canary I shall never know! I can tell you liked him Dear, didn't you!' addressing his comment to an unsuspecting middle-aged woman in the front row. 'I could see you were watching him ever so closely,' he added, his eyes now twinkling with mischief. 'Your mouth fell wide open when he wiggled his… Well, that's enough of that for now!'

The audience roared with laughter while the lady in the front row shrieked with embarrassment and buried her face in her hands.

'Now, Ladies and Gentlemen…' Marty announced loudly and slowly, and before the laughter had time to run its course, 'We have for you tonight… someone very special'.

There followed a short pause of comic timing to allow the audience to return to a receptive state.

'This young man is something else. He is going to go far and you are going to… *LOVE* him! Ladies and gentlemen, all the way from Chorley, and for the first time on *This Talented Isle,* I give you, Ladies and Gentlemen, the one and only, the *prodigious… JAMIE PARKIN.'*

Marty made an exaggerated sweeping gesture with his left arm as he spoke, leading the audience's attention away from himself and towards Jamie, who now walked calmly and confidently on to the stage. As he did so Marty turned to greet him, shook both of his hands at once, and made his exit while the curtains drew tantalisingly back to reveal the assorted props and mysterious paraphernalia of the act that was about to follow.

By now Abigail and Tony were almost beside themselves with a mixture of excitement and pride, tinged with dread in case anything should go wrong. Jamie, their youngest, had always been a bit of a showman and liked nothing more than to surprise people with the unexpected and the inexplicable. And now, here he was, on the telly for the first time. They had seen his act – or rather his various acts – on stage a number of times and he always did seem to have a particular way of building up and leading his audience in completely the wrong direction so that the finale would be full of surprise and have an even greater impact. After all, there are only so many magic tricks one can perform and Jamie had learned over many years from watching the greats that everything about success in this field lay in the particular personal touch that you brought to your act; the audience had to want to see you – not just the magic.

At the end of his twenty minute slot the audience broke into a rapturous applause, whooping and clapping and calling for more. His television debut had been a great success.

Meanwhile, however, his mother and father sat there and turned to each other, not so much enthralled as stunned and speechless.

Most of his act so far they had seen before but there was something about a well-primed television audience that lifted everything up to new heights. His parents were immensely proud and excited about just how much the audience loved his performance. Then came his finale.

After a suitable pause Jamie announced that he was

going to require the assistance of a member of the audience and scanned the front rows for a suitable candidate. Their expectations raised, the audience fell silent. After just the right amount of banter he settled on a young woman, Janice, newly-wed and blushing brightly at having to stand up in front of all these people and television cameras. But Jamie was already a master of putting people at their ease and, once on stage, she soon settled into it.

'Ladies and gentlemen,' Jamie continued, what none of you will know is that just before the show I gave six members of our audience twenty pounds each and asked them to buy a large box of chocolates. Would those six ladies please now stand up.'

'Ooooh!' Abigail beamed. 'We haven't seen this one before have we!'

Six female members of the audience rose slowly and expectantly to their feet.

'First of all, have you *all* managed to buy yourselves a box of chocolates?' Jamie asked.

The six women indicated that they had while the audience looked on expectantly.

'Excellent! May we see them please,' Jamie asked, and each of the women held up a box of chocolates for everyone to see. 'You haven't been eating them now, have you!'

There was a rumble of laughter at the very idea.

'Now then,' he said, turning to his right to speak to Janice. 'I want you, Janice, to tell me truthfully, do you know *any* of these ladies standing in the audience?'

She made it clear that she did not.

'OK, then!' he said, bringing his palms together in front of his mouth in a gesture of intense contemplation. 'What I want you to do is to choose one – any one – of these ladies, completely at random, to come up here, onto the stage with us. Can you do that for me?'

Janice chose a young, smartly-dressed woman standing near the aisle before being thanked warmly and invited to return to her seat.

In her place on the stage now stood Maria... from '*Espain*', though she spoke excellent English. Maria was twenty four years old and engaged to be married. 'Yes,' her fiancé was here with her and he was duly invited to stand up and show himself to the applauding audience.

'Maria, you have with you a brand new box of chocolates. Would you please show them to the audience.' Janice was once again called into play to confirm that the chocolates had not been tampered with and were still sealed in their clear cellophane wrapping. After a few more moments of apparently innocent conversation Jamie turned full on to the audience, guiding Maria by the left elbow to do the same.

'Maria, you've never met me before, have you... not until I gave you that twenty-pound note?'

'No.'

'And you have never met our lovely assistant, Janice before?' gesturing to the front row.

'No.'

'And you have in your right hand a brand new, unopened box of chocolates which you brought just before the show with the money I gave you?'

'I have.'

'Indeed, they are still in the original cellophane wrapping, are they not?

'Yes'

'Would you show these chocolates to the audience please... a little higher. Thank you.'

'Now, Maria, I am going to stand just over here, a couple of paces to your left, and what I would like you to do now is to open the box of chocolates and take a look inside. And just to be helpful, Maria... Ladies and Gentlemen... here is a small pair of scissors to help you to take off that difficult cellophane wrapping.' He passed her a small pair of scissors from his inside jacket pocket and stepped back again.

After the initial struggle the outer wrapping came off cleanly and Maria turned and smiled nervously at Jamie.

'It's fine,' he said. 'Go ahead and open the box and tell me what you see.

Maria lifted up the lid of the box so that it rose up between her and the audience. She then lifted the black inner cover and as she looked inside everyone could tell that she was clearly both puzzled and surprised. Suddenly she held out her left hand in front of her face and examined it. Splaying her fingers wide, she gasped with disbelief.

'Tell me what you see, Maria.'

'Oh my *God!*' she screamed, 'Ees not possible. This *cannot* be possible!'

She put her hand in the box, from which one chocolate was inexplicably missing, and from the empty well that remained, and between her right index finger and thumb, she took out something small, bright and shiny and examined it closely with an incredulous look.

'Ees my engagement ring!' she gasped and turned in astonishment to Jamie. 'How you *do* this?'

The audience stood up to applaud.

'Enjoy your chocolates,' Jamie said, having to raise his voice to complete the crescendo, 'and have a wonderful life together.'

Gesturing with both hands now towards his subject, Jamie announced, proudly and loudly:

'Ladies and Gentlemen, a big... *very* big warm hand please for... *MARIA!!!*'

3

The Unlucky Man

This is a re-telling of a traditional story that I first heard when I lived in Galicia.

Long ago, in a land far away and close to a big dark forest, lived a very unhappy man. He had never had a wife, his crops refused to grow, his dog ran away and, no matter how often he repaired it, his roof leaked every time it rained – which was often!

One day he went to the village to buy more nails to fix his roof and he soon found himself, once again, complaining to the people he met about how unlucky he was. At the village shop the shopkeeper listened patiently once more to his long tale of woe and bad luck. When he had finished he took the man to one side and suggested that he should seek out the wise old man who lived at the top of the high mountain on the far side of the forest.

'He is very wise,' he said. 'He knows everything and he is sure to be able to help you to improve your luck.'

So the man took his advice and the very next day he packed some food for the journey and set off from his little house and headed for the deep, dark forest. He knew it would be a difficult journey but, if the wise man at the top of the mountain could help him in some way to improve his luck, then it would be well worth it.

On the first morning nothing much happened. He walked

into the forest and it got darker and darker but the path was good and he made excellent progress. When at last he became hungry, he sat under a large oak tree where he ate bread and cheese and a large apple for his dinner. He soon finished his lunch and he was just about to resume his journey when he noticed a wolf watching him from behind a fallen tree.

'Good morning Mr Wolf,' said the man and the wolf came out of hiding to greet him. But he could see that this was no ordinary wolf; he looked very ragged and sickly and was so thin that his ribs protruded through his skin. His eyes were sunken and yellow and his legs were so shaky that they could hardly support his own weight.

'Where are you going?' asked the wolf. His voice was trembling.

'I am off on a journey to find the wise man at the top of the mountain,' replied the man. 'I am hoping that he will be able to improve my terrible luck.'

'Oh,' replied the wolf, 'I *so* wish I could come with you. But I am so weak now that I cannot even hunt for food anymore. Please ask him for me if he can change my bad luck too.'

'I will,' said the man and the two wished each other well as he went on his way.

The next day, when the man stopped for lunch, he sat once again beneath a large oak tree, but this tree was not at all well. Its leaves were going brown and starting to shrivel and some of its branches were dried and withered and were falling off. As the man sat and ate his lunch the tree spoke:

'Good morning,' it said to the man, making him jump.

The man leapt to his feet and looked at the tree. 'Good morning,' he replied.

'Are you travelling far?' asked the tree.

'Yes,' said the man, 'I am travelling to see the wise man that lives at the top of the mountain. I am hoping that he will be able to improve my terrible luck.'

'Oh!' replied the tree. 'I do *so* wish I could come with you but, of course, I am a tree and cannot walk.'

The man nodded, not quite sure what to say.

'I wonder…' added the tree. 'When you find him, would you please ask him how I can get better again. I have been so ill for so long.'

'I will,' said the man. They wished each other well and he continued once more on his journey.

The next day the man stopped again beneath a large tree for his lunch but met no-one. Then, after he had finished his lunch and continued on his journey, he soon came across a little thatched house in a clearing by the side of the path. At the front of the house, gathering herbs, stood a beautiful young woman. At first she looked very sad but, the moment she saw him, her face brightened into a lovely smile and she spoke:

'Good morning,' she said. 'Won't you stay for a while? It has been so long since I have spoken with anyone.'

'I am afraid not,' answered the man politely. 'I cannot stop because I am travelling to see the wise man who lives at the top of the mountain. I am hoping that he will be able to improve my terrible luck.'

'Oh,' said the young woman, looking quite sad now. 'I *so* wish I could come with you but I have to look after my animals. When you meet him would you please ask him for me how I can ever become happy again. I am so sad and lonely living here all on my own.'

'I will,' said the man and he doffed his hat and continued on his long journey.

It would be another three days' walking and climbing before the man reached the top of the mountain. But, at last, he knocked on the door of the wise old man.

The advice the old man gave was simple and clear:

'Your good luck is actually everywhere, all around you,' he said, 'It is already there, just waiting for you. All you need to do is to recognise it and take it when you see it.'

The traveller was truly overjoyed. This was better than he could have hoped for. His good luck was everywhere for the taking! He thanked the wise old man, bade him farewell, and with a spring in his step he set off home again the way he had come.

Three days later he once again met the beautiful young woman standing at the front of her lovely cottage, surrounded by flowers and fresh herbs.

'Good morning,' she said. Her face broke into a smile and she skipped over to meet him.

'Good morning,' he replied and stopped to talk to her.

'Did you meet the wise old man?' she asked eagerly.

'Indeed I did,' said the man. 'He told me that my good luck is all around me, everywhere, and that all I need to do is just to take it when I see it.'

'That's wonderful news,' she said. 'And did you ask him about me?'

'I did too,' said the man. 'He told me that all you need to do is to meet a man passing by your cottage and ask him to marry you. He said that you are so sweet and beautiful that no man could resist you and that when you find him you will never again be lonely or sad.'

'So, will *you* marry me?' she asked, blushing a little.

'Oh no, I'm afraid I cannot,' replied the man, shaking his head. 'I must be going for I am keen to find my good luck as soon as I can.' And with this he turned from her and walked off into the forest.

The young woman watched him sadly as he disappeared from view and from her life.

The next day the man came once more upon the sickly oak

tree and they greeted one another cheerfully.

'Good morning,' said the oak. 'Did you meet the wise old man?'

'I certainly did,' replied the man, 'and he was very helpful.'

'What did he say?' asked the oak.

'He told me that my good luck is all around me, everywhere, and that all I need to do is just to take it when I see it.'

'How wonderful,' the Oak replied. 'And did you ask him about me?'

'I did too,' said the man. 'He told me that you have a large casket of gold and silver buried among your roots and that this is the cause of all your troubles. If only you can find someone to dig this out and remove it he said that you would very quickly get better.'

'That is wonderful news,' said the oak. 'Please, *please* would you dig out the casket of gold and silver for me so that I can get better again.'

'Oh no, I'm afraid I cannot,' replied the man, shaking his head. 'I must be going for I am keen to find my good luck as soon as I can.' And with this he turned from the oak and walked off once more into the forest.

Another day passed and, once again, the traveller encountered the sickly wolf waiting by the side of the path.

'Oh good morning,' said the wolf. 'It's good to see you again.'

'Good morning to you,' said the man and stopped to talk.

'Did you meet the wise old man?' asked the wolf.

'I did,' replied the man, 'and he was most helpful.'

'What did he say?' asked the wolf.

'He told me that my good luck is all around me, everywhere, and that all I need to do is just to take it when I see it.'

'Oh, excellent news!' said the wolf. 'And did you ask him about me?'

'I did too,' the man replied.

The wolf was delighted. 'So what did he say?'

'He told me that all you need to do is to take the first person who is foolish enough to walk up to you... and eat him!'

4

Ryan's Story

My life and how I choose to live it is nobody's business but mine. That's what Sally, my social worker, said. Her actual name is Sally Firth but I call her Sally Forth because she's a scout leader. That's a joke. She's nice and she understands the problems I have, even when I get really frustrated and angry when things aren't right. That's the problem, you see. I'm absolutely fine as long as everything is right and as it should be and nobody starts changing things. But now I am getting better at that, as long as people explain what is going on and I know why I'm doing it. I used to get really upset and angry when people changed things about and they sent me to a special school for other kids like me. But of course they weren't like me. I'm the only one like me. You can't have two Me's… or twenty. Mum says that one Me is plenty, thank you very much. That's a joke as well. Most of the others kids at the school were more autistic than me. They were alright but they had their own interests and ways of doing things so it was easiest if I just did my own thing. The teachers tried to get me involved in all sorts of stuff and with the other kids but it didn't really work. Why would I do geography if I didn't *want* to do geography? Or cooking? That's just silly. But I liked maths. And I liked general science, especially electronic things. Maths was easy really and I liked the way the numbers popped up like a map or a diagram in my head so that I could just follow the diagram to find where the answer was. My teacher, Trudy (we called them all by their first names) said I was excellent at maths but I didn't like her. She liked to wear purple and I *hate* purple. It smells of horse poo.

Then, one day, another lady came to our school; Janet. They were nearly all women. She was a music therapist and she took an interest in me for some reason. At first she gave us drums and triangles and things to bang in rhythm and things to blow, simple stuff, and then one day I was watching her play the piano and I asked if I could have a go and she let me. And that was it. It was brilliant how a tune would just come into my head – something I had heard somewhere before – and then it would just come out of my fingers and into the piano and then back out again. Just as I had heard it in the first place. Then she gave me some sheet music – lots of dots and squiggles on the page – and when she explained what the different notes were it all made perfect sense. So I could just look at the page and the music just came out and I didn't seem to be doing anything much really. But I loved doing it. I really loved the music and it was *me* creating it almost out of nowhere. Then lots of other people wanted to hear me play as well. And I was even on television. The One Show. I had no idea what all the fuss was about.

Then, one day, Joe, my sister's boyfriend, played me some jazz and that was something completely different. It was fantastic but he also told me that to do it really well you had to be able to improvise and that was a strange idea at first. No sheet of music or memory of a tune telling you what notes to play or when to play them. But then I thought, 'OK'. And from then on it just started to grow inside me. As long as I understood what I was meant to be doing the music would just come out of me. Later, Joe introduced me to a couple of friends of his from university, Freddie and Michelle. They were a bit older than him, and then we were joined by Jerry on the double bass... he's got an enormous nose, and we all started to play together and soon we were performing gigs. We call ourselves Blue Wind. We're playing in London tonight – a big one – quite a bit of money too. I'm going to buy my mum a food mixer. Sally says that's a really nice idea.

5

A Nice Cup of Tea

If you were looking for a great time in Shenton then Brenda's Café, down at the far end of Market Street, was definitely not the place for you. The décor (I use the term advisedly) was old and faded, if always spotlessly clean, and the furniture was an *ad hoc* assortment of second-hand tables and chairs; cheap, Formica-topped or veneered, often wobbly, but serviceable. Here Brenda served up only the basics: steaming-hot builders' tea (cup or mug); bacon; sausages; beans and pies; egg on toast, and the like, and the coffee was from a simple filter machine… none of your espressos or flat whites or cappuccinos here with their silly fern-leaf patterns. Consequently the young people of the town, with their expensive iPhones and tablets and their estuarine-chic, were more than happy to take their custom elsewhere.

On the other hand I really liked the place, partly for its sheer unpretentiousness, but also for the fact that it was friendly, cheap, and conveniently close to where I worked. It also happened to be next door to the newsagents, which was partly what brought me there on that grey Thursday last November.

I had been there many times before, but always avoided the bustle and the noise of market days, and by now Brenda and I were on warm and friendly chatting terms. We had little in common as such, she being from a market family and I a teacher of economics, but she had a terrific sense of humour and such a cheery and welcoming way about her that our conversations were always friendly and entertaining.

Today I was a little earlier than usual as things at work had been brought forward this afternoon. So the place was quiet… empty in fact, save for a young, nervous-looking woman tucked away on her own in the dim light of the far left-hand corner. As always, I brought my own newspaper with me. I didn't need to order; I always had the same thing and I took my favourite seat near the door and by the window where the light was good.

Moments later, Brenda brought over my mug of steaming tea, commenting jokingly, 'Our rotten old rag not good enough for you, then?' and she tilted her head slightly to try to catch the upside down headlines of my Guardian.

I said something inconsequential, smiled a friendly, 'Thanks Brenda,' and unfolded my newspaper, reaching for my tea with my right hand as I did so. The smell of bacon already on the go was a delightful distraction, almost as though it were calling my name, and I skimmed the first couple of pages inattentively, looking for something more arresting than the smell of bacon and the usual political shenanigans and depressing economic forecasts.

Two or three pages in, something caught my eye and I took a careful sip of hot tea and put my mug back down without lifting my eyes from the page. It wasn't so much the headline that held my attention; 'Police Search Continues for Murder Suspect', so much as the photograph which – resisting the temptation now to look up and stare – bore a remarkable resemblance to the anxious-looking young woman sitting in the far corner, not ten paces from where I was sitting.

When Brenda eventually brought a large bacon roll to my table, the accompanying clatter of plates and knives and forks caused us both to look up momentarily so that the young woman and I made brief eye contact. It was *her*, I was absolutely sure of it, but she instantly lowered her gaze and set about nervously chewing her bottom lip.

'There you go Sweetheart,' said Brenda, smiling, and a brief chat ensued about what I was up to this week, about my ongoing manuscript, and how her Sid – who had been a publican in his time – also wrote a book once… all about his shadier days as a young man in the East End.

'Any brown sauce love?'

This brief exchange allowed me another fleeting glimpse at the young woman and, once more, she snatched a nervous glance in my direction. But she was clearly unsettled by my presence and immediately lowered her eyes again, looking down determinedly into her empty teacup.

I thanked Brenda and she flipped her tea towel casually over her shoulder and moved on to the young woman's table in the far corner. Straight away she hunched over her, with her back to me, and the pair fell into hushed conversation. At one point she looked back to me, as though they had been talking about me, and then, beaming her usual smile, she picked up her empty side-plate and tea cup and returned to the front of the café. But I noticed, as she passed by, how she caught my eye and gave me an odd but knowing look; serious, slightly conspiratorial perhaps. She obviously knew the young woman and seemed to be involved with her in some odd way.

As the place fell quiet again the walls seemed to close in on me a little and I set about my bacon roll while I continued reading the article: an abusive and violent husband with criminal connections, stabbed in the back of the neck while he slept off a skin-full-and-a-half of alcohol; a large and missing stash of drug-money; his missing partner, now the main suspect;

gangland associates... also looking for her! As yet, no-one had any clues as to her whereabouts and there had been no word or contact at all since her disappearance six days ago.

Starting to feel anxious myself now, I sneaked another brief look at her. She was unkempt... and was that the remaining yellow shadow of a black eye? I couldn't be sure in that light.

On the wall immediately behind her she was framed by a large and fading poster; one of those mock bullfight posters which people bring back personalised from the south of Spain. In this case the celebrated matador was 'El Sid'... Brenda's deceased husband no doubt. What is it about the British and their almost insatiable love of corny puns!

My thoughts were suddenly interrupted by a loud 'PING' and I almost jumped in my seat as the door behind me opened and someone entered the café; a man... I could tell from his footfall as he entered and approached the counter. I didn't look up. Behind me, he and Brenda spoke in a whisper for a few seconds and then he walked over to the far corner, a glass of water in his hand, to join the young woman. She looked hugely relieved to see him and shuffled across to allow him to sit next to her. He wore an expensive grey suit with a relaxed and casual air, enhanced by the designer sunglasses, which he now hooked by one arm over the neck of his black tee shirt.

The pair settled into quiet conversation as Brenda brought what looked like a cheese roll to the table. She, too, joined in the conversation for a few more seconds before making her way back to the counter again. Clearly preoccupied, she hardly looked at me this time. The couple ignored the cheese roll completely.

By now I had finished my early lunch and couldn't stay. Curiosity or no, I had to get back to work. But, as I folded my paper and went to stand up, there was another loud PING at the door and another man walked in. Half-turned in my seat by now, I saw him briefly look around till his eyes settled, with an unmistakable air of cold menace, upon the couple in the far corner.

They stood up suddenly to face him, she with a look of shock on her face, he serious while remaining calm and chillingly self-assured.

'Alby!' he pronounced, matter-of-factly.

'Jimmy!', the stranger responded, likewise.

As Alby took a single threatening step forward, Jimmy loosened his jacket and I gasped as I caught sight of the grey handle of a pistol protruding, with that same casual presence, from the waistband of his trousers.

At this point I froze – both inside and out – and thought for a second that I might wet myself.

But in that instant, and before anyone could make another move, there was a dull thud behind me as Brenda calmly placed a shotgun on the counter with the barrel lined-up roughly in Alby's direction. She spoke like I'd never heard her before:

'We'll have none of this in here, Alby Price, you know that!'

Suddenly, cheerful, amiable Brenda had taken on all the cold and calculated determination of a gangland fixer.

'You wouldn't have done this in my Sid's day,' she added, 'and you won't do it in mine!'

Her face was unblinking, set cool and hard, almost daring him to make another move. My quiet lunch break had turned into a three-cornered, armed stand-off, with me as sole spectator and, as likely as not, about to become listed in the news as an 'innocent bystander'.

Alby, still chancing the odds, moved to take another step forward but was further checked by Brenda who raised her eyebrows in grim warning and then lifted the shotgun, still waist-high, and pointed it straight at him.

By now I was utterly terrified. The silence physically hurt my chest, as though I was being crushed by some huge, hungry python, and I looked up expectantly, frantically towards Brenda.

She quietly stood her ground, her eyes fixed on her opponent, cool and unflinching, ready to do battle.

'You'll not harm one of mine, Alby!' she warned.

For sure, Alby's life hung in the balance now and it was clear in his face that he knew Brenda was not going to back down.

Jimmy, in the far corner, looked on, silent, still, cool and unblinking… but spring-loaded and ready to deliver.

Nothing, and no-one, moved for what seemed like half a minute until Brenda chanced one cautious eye back in my direction, and then from me towards the door as she announced, calmly:

'On the house, love!'

6

The Doghouse Chronicles

I knew that look straight away and it said trouble. She didn't say anything; she didn't have to. I had simply walked headlong into another of those *doghouse* moments and experience told me that I was going to have to tread carefully for the time being, at least until things shifted back onto the more productive terrain of the conversational. And this could take some time.

'What's the matter?' I asked, not really expecting much by way of an answer.

'Nothing,' she replied with that air of almost malevolent indifference that she had polished to such perfection over our twenty one years together. Passive aggression hardly described it; when she was like this she could unsettle a rhinoceros and, with similar reservations, I knew that it was best not to tackle her head on.

So I said nothing. I drew in a deep breath, turned and went to hang up my jacket and change into my slippers. Patience and a calm approach were needed here, but first I needed a few moments to rise above these recurring feelings of bewilderment and frustration. The words, *'Here we go again!'* were whizzing round and round in my head like an angry wasp and I needed to silence them before I could deal with the situation. I could see her from where I sat thinking in the living room, or rather I could see her reflection in the glass door, her neat pale blue apron and pink washing up gloves to protect her hands and her nails, quietly washing up and then rinsing each item under the warm tap, placing them neatly into the rack… ever so neatly. That was her way.

My heart had sunk but I wasn't angry with her, not *properly* angry anyway. In spite of it all: the constant rows; the accusations; the long punishing silences; the sexual Badlands; I knew what was happening and that helped. It also helped that I still loved her. She was a good looking woman and it's true that I've always had an eye for an attractive woman. Even now, with her greying hair, the thinning lips, the beautiful figure – more milk bottle now than hourglass I admit – I was still attracted to her and wanted her. She was kind and loving too, at least while she was on an even keel. But these difficult mood swings seemed to be occurring more frequently lately and I really wanted to understand why.

Back in the kitchen, facing her side-on, I asked her what was happening.

Silence! No… more than that; it was though I wasn't there!

So I spoke again, as gently and as reasonably as I possibly could:

'Listen Love, something's wrong and we have to *talk*. Nothing will get sorted like this.'

A fleeting, sideways flash of her eye acknowledged my presence, followed by a brief moment of stillness. Then she drew in her breath and turned quickly to face me. Raising a stiff arm she pointed accusingly to the table on the far side of the room and then, just as quickly, turned back to the sink.

I was curious now… that was good, better than anger or frustration anyway. And certainly better than these awful Arctic silences. Looking at the table, though, I could see nothing untoward and turned back to Jennifer at the sink. But she was determined not to give anything more away so I walked over to the table to take a closer look.

Apart from the daffodils, which were now just on the turn, the only item of any interest was my wallet which I picked up unthinkingly, still uncertain as to what might be wrong here. Only as it fell open in my hand did anything of interest catch my eye. It was stuffed with money... *lots* of money. There must have been near-on five hundred pounds in there. But it was the two pieces of paper that fell out onto the table which most attracted my attention. A neat business card lay face up, pretty pink with a red flowery border, and, as I edged it round with my index finger to read it better, my curiosity turned quickly to astonishment. Stunned, I said nothing for a moment or two but just stared aghast at the wording on the card:

Goody Two Shoes
Exotic Dancer
Personal Services.
Discretion guaranteed.

'What the...!'

Picking up the card I turned full-on to Jennifer at the sink. She shot me a murderous glance, noticed that I had not yet opened the piece of paper, and waggled her hand dismissively at me before briskly turning her back on me once more. With some trepidation now I picked up the piece of folded paper and opened it. But it made little sense. Apart from some pairs of capital letters, alongside some numbers – names, dates and times I imagined – the rest seemed to be in some kind of code and gave nothing at all away. The page itself had been torn from a small A5 pad and the code consisted of about a dozen lines of seemingly random letters assembled into neat groups of six. For sure, *someone* was up to something. But it sure as hell wasn't me!

'What on earth *IS* this?' I demanded.

Jennifer said nothing immediately. Instead she stopped what she was doing and, gripping the edge of the sink with both hands, tensed and went rigid with anger.

In that moment, as I paused and looked at her back, the penny began to drop. Before I could speak, however, she turned to face me with a look that could have downed a flock of birds in flight.

'This had better be good!' Arms folded tightly, she gave the impression that she was trying her level best not to physically attack me where I stood.

I put the piece of paper back on the table and picked up the wallet with my right hand, flapping it loosely in the air in front of me.

'It's not mine,' I said. 'I don't know whose it is... but it's *not mine!* Look, I'll show you.'

Tossing the wallet onto the table I walked out of the kitchen and retrieved my own wallet from my jacket pocket.

'Here. *See!* This is mine. I've no idea whose that one is. Where did you find it?'

The two wallets were virtually identical save for their contents and it was easy to see how they might be mistaken for one another.

I picked up the calling card from the table and added, 'And this *certainly* isn't mine. What *were* you thinking!'

Part of me felt disappointed at her lack of trust in me but I knew only too well the extraordinary difficulties that she faced when it came to trust. And then sadness as I watched her almost crumple on the spot, like one of those Muffin the Mule toys we used to get after the War, the ones where you pressed in the base and the toy figure collapsed in on itself, only to spring back again when you let go.

The hug we shared was also a kind of a collapse; the

incredible release of tension, the coming back together again, the hot tears, the comforting words, her choked apologies, the kisses, the reassurances.

'I found it down the back of the settee,' she said afterwards and pointed to the place where Phil and Harriet had sat the evening before.

'Phil?' we both uttered in unison and in disbelief.

'Oh *no!'* Jenny gasped, covering her mouth with cupped hands.

This was nothing short of a disaster! Phil, Jennifer's half-brother, was the only other man I knew that she fully trusted and was able to get close to. This was a huge setback for her.

7

Winner Takes All

Michael sipped his sweet, milky tea nervously while staring blankly at the couple sitting at a nearby table. Pinching the heavy white cup with its too-tiny handle between thumb and forefinger, he steadied it with those of the left hand in a kind of pincer movement. He had learned that drinking like this, with his elbows firmly on the table and his feet flat on the floor, he was less likely to spill his drink during his moments of involuntary movement or shaking.

After a while he slipped into an animated conversation with himself, too quiet at first for others to hear, but then he began to raise his voice slightly and people started to notice him:

'Shouldn't be any crabs,' he was saying. 'There aren't any crabs here. People don't like them you see. They don't like the crabs, especially the big ones. I don't like the big ones.'

Almost straight away Maura, the pretty young waitress with purple hair and a silver stud in her nose, appeared at his table.

'You alright, Michael?'

'Yes, thank you, I'm alright. I'm alright... Yes,' he stuttered in reply. He made no eye contact but continued to stare into the middle distance while the couple at the nearby table politely distracted themselves with the menu.

Maura always kept a kindly eye out for Michael when it was her shift as his occasional outbursts could unsettle the clientele a bit, though he was always friendly and polite and never aggressive in any way. Sometimes she even forgot to charge him for his drink.

'I don't like the crabs, you see,' he repeated.

'I know,' said Maura reassuringly. 'But there aren't any crabs here are there, not even in the sandwiches.' And she laughed, which put him at his ease.

Crab sandwiches were a favourite along this stretch of the south coast… only not at this café, where cooked food was more the order of the day. And, actually, it was still a little early, even for that.

Maura brought Michael a couple of biscuits on a plate.

'There you are, Michael. Let me know if you need anything else.'

'Thank you,' said Michael, making eye contact for the first time.

It was twenty years almost to the day since his friend Simon took up his challenge down by the beach. Overdriven with excess testosterone and strong cider, and giddy with the heat of the midsummer sun, Michael thought it would be a great idea to have a race along the Dumbles.

Simon was far less certain.

The Dumbles was a perilous place and ordinarily it would be fenced off, with large red enamel signs warning the public to stay clear. Only last year an experienced angler had lost his life on the rocks down there. Recently, however, a group of bored youngsters had torn back the fence with graffiti in mind. Their canvas was the long stretch of sheer cliff-face that ran from just above the western end of the main beach down towards Dendry Bay, a mile and a half further on. At the base of the cliff, and for about half its length, a narrow and rocky shingle beach hissed and slurped like a sleeping monster with each wave, while about twenty feet above ran a long narrow ledge, just wide enough for two people at best.

'You race, I'll watch,' responded Simon dismissively. He knew he was fast on his feet, and probably a good match for Michael on the flat, but he was much more concerned about the dangers of venturing, let alone racing along the ledge. There were narrow stretches and others that were sloping, uneven and slippery and, at the far end, shortly before the path came to an abrupt halt, there was a gully to be jumped where the sea rumbled in, wild and angry, some twenty feet or so below.

'You're crazy! It's bloody dangerous along there!' he added.

Michael, not to be put off, goaded him with chicken noises; *'Buk, buk! Buk, buk! Buuuuuk, buk, buk!'* And when Simon shook his head at him he continued even louder.

'Bugger off!' Simon retorted, getting more than a little cross at his persistence.

When the goading continued their friend Chris chipped in. He and Ollie had sat there without comment up until now:

'Look, just *do* it!' he gasped in frustration, 'if only to shut the stupid sod up! You don't even have to race it. Just go through the motions and let him have his day.'

Ollie was nodding in agreement and the pair looked at each other rolling their eyes skywards. What the hell was it with some of these guys? For some stupid reason they constantly seemed to need to put themselves and everyone else to the test.

Chris lit a cigarette, still shaking his head.

As for Mikey, he just wouldn't let up, even when the answer was no; it was as though something deeply personal depended on it. At times like this he could be a pain in the jacksy!

So when Simon finally thumped his drink down on the table and muttered, 'Right, come on then.' it was already beginning to feel like a bit of a hollow victory for Michael.

Ollie went off to get the drinks while Chris continued to

look on disdainfully and took a long drag of his cigarette as the two friends set off towards the cliff.

At the start, just the other side of the broken fence, Michael checked his watch. Moments later they set off and, taking no prisoners, he took the lead almost immediately. Even if Simon's heart wasn't in it Michael was determined to make this his personal best, wrenching some kind of victory at least from a somewhat ignominious start.

The first stretch was easy, level and plenty wide enough for two, even though Michael sensed already that he was only racing himself. But Simon wasn't far behind and he could hear him quite clearly, causing him to put on an extra spurt so as to get to the narrower section before him. Soon the path began to slope downwards a little towards the beach and the going became uneven and more slippery underfoot. But still Michael kept up the pressure. The path widened again a little further on and he wanted to be sure that he wasn't going to lose his advantage.

Around the midway point Michael checked his watch again. He was about five seconds up on his previous time and, feeling elated now, he put everything into the final half. Soon the track sloped upwards quite steeply but he covered this section with no great effort and by the time it levelled out again he could no longer hear Simon at his heels and he knew he was way ahead. Perhaps he wasn't trying but... *'What the hell!'* By the time he reached the mouth of the gully, some two hundred yards further on, a quick check of his watch told him that he had probably knocked another couple of seconds off his previous time. Feeling great he followed the cliff-face round to the right where the path ran along above the gully towards the narrow point near the end where he could jump across to the far side.

This was by far the most dangerous bit. From here there

was a long sheer drop down to the rocks below where the sea rolled in, heaving itself up violently like some monstrous ram before crashing headlong like thunder into the rocks at the wedge-end of the gulley.

Michael paused for a brief moment for the largest wave and its cloud of spray to subside, and then he was across. Racing back along the other side of the gulley he reached the mouth again where a quick look to his left and back along the path showed no signs of his friend. Twenty yards further on he reached the end where the track suddenly butted up against a sheer outcrop of rock. He had won! Nearly six seconds down on the last time he did it.

On his way back along the track he began to think more clearly about Simon. He was a good friend; he liked him a lot, and now the excitement was over he slightly regretted goading him. He would buy him a drink when he got back and smooth things over.

Back at the table, outside the pub, Michael was greeted by Chris and Ollie, not looking at all impressed.

'Well?' they insisted together. 'Well, who won then? And where's Simon?'

'I thought he'd turned back,' replied Michael, 'Haven't you seen him?'

From the tables there was a clear view of the damaged fence from where Simon ought have appeared, had he turned back.

'Of course we haven't seen him,' retorted Ollie, 'Otherwise, why would we ask!' There was a cross note of anxiety in his voice and now the three boys looked at each other with worried faces.

Having found no trace of Simon back at the Dumbles, Chris called him but couldn't get through, so he took the decision to call his father, with whom he lived. Michael was, by now, looking grey and much the worse for wear. But Simon had not come home and now everyone was worried. Chris didn't mention the boys' race along the Dumbles to his father, but he did to the police when they finally reported him missing. The expression on the desk sergeant's face said everything.

Simon did not return. His body was not found until almost a week later, three miles further along from where his race ended, when a freak wave had sucked him off the lower section of the cliff-face like an oyster from its shell.

Michael became withdrawn and depressed even before the news broke, but when the gory details of the discovery reached him it was as though the very breath of life had drained out of him. The stories that followed gave ghoulish accounts of the condition of his friend's ravaged and broken remains and of crabs and other creatures of the seabed crawling from his mouth and his eye sockets.

Soon afterwards, Michael was sucked down into his own dark and dismal depths and there he remained for the rest of his life until pneumonia took him, like a kindly friend, in middle-age.

8

Love for Beginners

When Steve woke up with a hangover the next morning his first thought was of Anna, which was unusual for him; where specific members of the opposite sex were concerned it was usually a case of *here today, gone tomorrow... out of sight, out of mind!* But today he had the feeling that he really wanted to see her again. Except that it was so fleeting that it was hardly a feeling at all really, just a very small butterfly in his stomach and then, almost immediately, the anger welled up in him and he was calling her a stuck-up cow all over again.

Sure, he really fancied her when he first saw her in the Two Brewers last week and he even said as much to Tony, though his mate was singularly unimpressed and commented that she had a face 'like a bloody horse'. Unperturbed, Steve found a chance to get talking to her and bought her a drink... ginger beer, very unusual but quite a useful conversation starter for that.

She did drink alcohol apparently, but only at weekends. It was a healthier option and she liked to keep her head clear for work the next day; teaching assistant, very tiring sometimes, and it didn't pay very well, but she loved working with the children and wanted to train up properly.

Without realising it, Steve had found himself chatting to a *'classy chick'* and he felt that he needed to play this one a bit carefully. She was nice and she even seemed quite interested in him, which was great. They had some things in common too, not the football or the wild drinking of course but, like him, she liked to fly off to the sun when she could, and especially to Tenerife, which just happened to be one of Steve's favourite good-time haunts. Not Playa de las Américas, though. Somewhere in the north of the island that he had never heard of, where her parents had a villa. And it even had its own swimming pool. He was well-in here!

As they chatted the bar filled up and got noisier and hotter and conversation became a bit more difficult. There were frequent outages now so that Steve and she had to converse almost cheek to cheek in order to be heard. As they got closer to one another he could smell her and feel her bodily warmth, and once or twice his face brushed against her hair where it hung loosely over her right ear. And with each moment of contact he found himself wanting it to happen again.

Eventually he popped the question:

'It's getting a bit noisy in here. D'you fancy going somewhere a bit quieter?'

Anna drew back momentarily from their common space in order to look at him, her eyes both knowing and questioning at the same time. 'What... like another bar?'

'If you like,' said Steve, but he had given the game away in the tone of his voice. Her eyes said so. Obviously he was not about to pull here but, equally, he didn't want her to get away either and he did what he could to recover the lost ground. For some strange reason he really liked her, which was new territory for Steve and he wasn't at all sure of the rules.

Soon they got ready to leave the bar and Steve gave the statutory wink, if a little awkwardly, to Tony on the way out.

At Rafael's they talked some more over *calamare* and *pimientos de Padrón*... lager for him, white wine and soda for her. *Pushing the boat out,* Steve observed, surely a good sign! And they enjoyed the conversation and laughed a lot, and for a short while they even held hands across the table. But it soon became clear to Steve that sex was not on the menu that night. On the other hand Anna, checking her watch, agreed quite happily to meet him again on Friday night. In fact she said she'd like that, which made him feel strangely elated, and they agreed on a Thai curry, or an Indian, somewhere a little special.

When it came to making love that Sunday afternoon Steve felt, at first, oddly excited but uncomfortable too, all at the same time. To be more exact, it was Anna who had love-making in mind while Steve found himself in a complete emotional turmoil. Sex was one thing, and he would always 'rise to the occasion', so to speak, like a true performer. But *making love* – slowly, gently, sweetly – this was something else and soon pushed him way out of his comfort zone. For Anna, making love involved reciprocity and taking your time, it involved mutual tenderness and caring, giving as well as being given in to, even relinquishing control, all of which made him feel desperately vulnerable. The idea of completely losing himself in another was to drown in a maelstrom of unfamiliar and frightening feelings. And clearly there was to be no quick escape to safety as soon as he'd finished either.

After their disappointingly… for her, brief encounter, Steve lay on his back, lost for words, not wanting her to become upset and certainly not wanting to lose her, but also distracted and irritated now by missing the Arsenal match on TV. Conversation on his part became sporadic and monosyllabic until eventually he excused himself to go to the loo. He had broken the uncomfortable impasse between them but, in so doing, he finally extinguished any traces of that mysterious reverie that helps to mark out love from the mere act of sex.

Downstairs the tension between them soon became palpable and part of Steve felt slightly relieved when Anna said that she needed to get home. She had things to prepare for work in the morning, she said.

As she spoke he felt he needed to turn his face from her. He was frightened she might see his real feelings in his eyes and in the tell-tale muscles of his face, even though he himself was barely able to recognise these for what they were.

Anna didn't call him or text the next day, or the next, and by Wednesday Steve was feeling awful. He really wanted to see her again and became restless, tetchy and unable to concentrate until eventually, early that evening, he took himself off somewhere quiet and dialled her number.

Anna's response was non-committal, not cold or angry, more polite – which was even worse – as she told him that she felt it would be better if they just left things where they were. She liked him, she said, reassuringly, but it just wasn't for her.

'Yeah, fine,' said Steve.

But is wasn't.

'See ya then.'

'Sure, see you.'

That night, down at the local and all on his own, he got smashed out of his face.

9

Beeswing

Thursday morning, 6.35: sunny; cool… at least according to the radio forecast; rain on the way; tube strike, and talks were making no more headway than the trains themselves. Phone the dentist.

Robert had come downstairs at the exact same time almost every day for the past sixteen years and there was no reason whatsoever why today should be any different. He was a creature of habit, always had been; dependable, responsible and hard-working… if more tortoise than hare.

Some say that it is the plodders of this world who stay the course; was it the poet, Robert Service who said that? He wasn't sure. And, although he wasn't exactly a wealthy man, he had done very well. Both of the children were now at university, the house was all paid for, and certainly spacious and comfortable enough, and he had his 'pride and joy', his two-sleeper Volkswagen campervan in which he could take off on his own when the mood suited him, do a bit of walking, some bird-watching, enjoy the peace and quiet… all far away from the City, the polluted air and the crowds.

Was he happy? Well, that depends! He was certainly contented. And there are different kinds of 'happy' anyway, aren't there: there's the kind where you almost wake up singing each day, only it tends not to last… and it drives everyone else potty after a while; and there's the kind where all the appearances point to 'happy' – the dancing and the drinking, the gaiety and the fun of the party – but it often seems more surface-dressing than anything resembling a state of inner bliss, and then there's the happiness that glows – sometimes brighter, sometimes a little less so – but it sustains you like your very own inner sunshine, along with those who are fortunate enough to share it with you.

So, was Robert happy? Well, none of the above, that's for sure. Happy enough? Perhaps… or was this just the absence of unhappiness! Either way, he didn't spend much time thinking about such things. Today, like any other day, he had to get to work, and today, once again, it would be by bike.

He left a little earlier this morning, as he had done for the past two weeks, and he spent his day much as he had done in all the years that he had been there. He worked his way meticulously through several sets of accounts with nothing much amiss… though Faraday's were a complete mess, received and made the usual phone calls… including the dentist, had a meeting with Henry Armitage from Calver's Holdings, then a hurried sandwich for lunch and, probably, one cup of tea too many; his bladder seemed a little weaker these days and he would need to be sure to go to the loo before any meetings or long phone calls.

And then, homeward once more on the trusty bike, through the spray and the noise and the stinking traffic, sworn at by impatient motorists and scowled at by others. But he made it home intact, locked up his bike behind the side gate, and opened the front door, stooping to pick up the post as he entered.

In the kitchen he tossed the mail onto the table, took off his beanie hat and showerproof jacket, and then sat down to take off his cycle clips and to put on his slippers. Then he stood up again to put the kettle on.

Seven items in all: three circulars… straight into the

recycling box; the bank; council tax; car service due, and a postcard...

The tea was instantly forgotten.

The views were of somewhere in the South of France – Provence at a guess – but he couldn't work out the postmark. Colourful pictures of a large farmhouse at the end of long straight rows of purple Lavender; a wide languid river; a bustling market; a picturesque village nestling on a hill, and the message on the other side was short and to the point:

Still love you.
Dx
All my love to the kids.

Darcy had been the love of his life... his only love in fact, not being of a passionate disposition, and she was about as different from him as she could be. She was wispish, wild and free, and her long, dark hair and loose-layered clothes would swirl around her like mist as she glided from place to place, half-skipping, half-dancing, or playing her fiddle and singing along with the birds of Spring.

She didn't work... she couldn't work – any more than you could put a butterfly to work – and her place on this Earth was much as any rose or violet or forget-me-not, and she would spread her love around in much the same way, asking nothing, giving freely of herself, as happy and as free as a bird.

She and Robert had two lovely children, whom she named Sky and Juliet, and she doted upon them lovingly and selflessly, not caring one jot about the mess they made, or the porridge smeared round their mouths, or whether or not they were wearing any clothes, but taking every opportunity to giggle, and tickle, to roll around and laugh, to kiss and cuddle and feed and caress. The love poured out of her ceaselessly like a clear sweet waterfall. And then, one warm day in late Spring, she was gone.

The children by now were aged four and nearly-three and, one Sunday morning, while Robert was reading the newspaper in bed, she brought him a mug of hot tea, packed a few things and left him and the children behind, without warning or explanation. All she left was a drawer full of winter clothes and the briefest note:

So sorry, have to go.
Love you lots.
Dx

That was sixteen years ago and there hadn't been a single word since. Robert, of course, held the fort in his ever-reliable way, and loved the kids and cooked and cleaned and sent them off to school, always well-dressed and prepared, though he did need to pay someone to help out so that he could continue going to work every day. And thus life carried on – emptier than before, certainly – but good for all that.

He picked up the card and read it again and then he cried for the first time in sixteen years; sobs and tears that seemed to come from some dark, bottomless hole beneath as he flopped, helpless, on the settee, with his head in his hands, and just let go of everything that held him together. It would be a good ten minutes before he could even begin to compose himself.

A short while later, he turned off the water and the gas, took his keys, locked up the house and left.

He was found a week later by a dog-walker, hunched over the wheel of his wrecked campervan. The police presumed that he had left the road during heavy rain and plunged into a steep gulley, nearly five hundred miles from his home. Perhaps he'd fallen asleep. Nobody really knew.

Back at the house the police found nothing to suggest that it might have been anything other than an unfortunate accident, just the postcard on the kitchen table, along with a few hurried lines from a song by Richard Thompson… one of Darcy's all-time favourite songwriters. It was a song that Robert had played almost constantly since the day she left and the same disk was found in the CD player of his crashed campervan:

> *She was a rare thing*
> *Fine as a beeswing*
> *So fine a breath of wind might blow her away*
> *She was a lost child*
> *She was running wild.*
> *She said, as long as there's no price on love, I'll stay*
> *And you wouldn't want me any other way.*

Beeswing,
Words and music
by Richard Thompson.

10

Boys and Girls

Not so long ago, on a beautiful Spring morning, bright with warm sunshine and alive with colour and birdsong, I was on my way to the park for my usual walk with Sam, our good-natured border collie. *Will there be sticks?* I could almost hear him ask as he bounced happily and expectantly alongside me. There would of course be sticks. Today was going to be a good day for both of us, you could just feel it in the air.

Merlin Avenue, where we lived at that time, could hardly be described as leafy suburbia yet it was a lovely place to be, where children played happily and safely in the street and where kindly neighbours kept a constant look-out for them and for each other. In fact our street was such a sociable place to live that it was even starting to become reflected in the property prices as word-of-mouth reached young families looking for a new home. Fortunately for us as well, we lived on the south-facing side of the street, which provided an additional bonus in that it drew so many passers-by in our direction with their general chit-chat and local news; just one of the many ways in which we kept a close neighbourly eye out for one another.

During our time there it had become established that the half-dozen or so younger children from further along the street were allowed to play out only so far as *Sam's House,* where cheerful Sam obligingly hung over the low sandstone wall, attracting the maximum of fuss and attention, though never actually jumping over to join them. So it was that, on any dry morning during weekends and school holidays, you might hear the chattering of children's voices as they arrived outside to play with him, though of course we always kept a very close eye on them... a dog is always a dog, after all!

On this particular morning, just a short way down the street, I met one of our neighbours standing outside her house with her three young children, all devoted fans of Sam. And it was a sight to take your breath away.

The eldest girl, aged about eight, was as strikingly pretty as any young girl could ever hope to be. With her fair skin and rosy cheeks, her long, tumbling fair curls and big crystal-blue eyes, she could have risen up out of any fairy tale. Next to her, her young sister was every bit as pretty, only in a different way. Aged only four, she was the youngest child, dark-haired and still very much the infant as she gazed inquisitively back at you with her large, innocent, questioning eyes, as big and brown as conkers.

By way of contrast, the middle child, Anthony, aged about six, had already abandoned *cute* for those more rumbustious boyish ways. He was much more active and outgoing and could fire questions at you till your head ached. They were adorable children, happy, polite, sweet-natured and inquisitive – especially Anthony – and they were regular visitors to our front gate where they could be heard cooing over Sam.

This morning, however, it was the girls themselves who were being cooed over. Today, even though it was still quite early, their mother had dressed them up picture-book-pretty in brand-new matching outfits. Their identical dresses, richly embroidered and brightly-coloured, had been made to fit them perfectly and were lifted to absolute perfection by the girls' neatly-brushed hair, their colourful bows and hair-slides and the prettiest new red shoes imaginable. So stunning were they that on this lovely April morning the flowers of spring went almost unnoticed.

Just before my arrival, their beaming mother had been joined by a small assortment of adoring neighbours and passers-by who now heaped rapturous admiration and praise upon the blushing girls, as well as upon their mother of course, for having such 'beautiful, *beautiful daughters!*' And as the compliments gushed out of them, they would soon start to run out of adequate words of adulation and so resort to repeating their mellifluous praises over and over again, interspersing these with assorted longings and pleas, beseeching their mother... *Please! Please!* that these two adorable girls should be allowed to come back home with them.

In response to their neighbours' questions the girls shyly volunteered that the dresses had been made especially for them by their Nana... who lived near Chester... eliciting further outpourings of praise and wonder as to how lucky they were to have *'such a clever and lovely Nana'*, and causing the already blushing girls to bury themselves even more deeply and coyly into their mother's side.

No mother could have been prouder of her daughters than she at that moment, and no two girls could have been more rightly and highly praised and admired for their sweetness, their sheer charm and their beauty. It was a delightful scene to witness.

And yet, not three feet behind them, and entirely unnoticed, their bewildered brother, Anthony, seemed almost to have ceased to exist and now, not knowing what else to do with himself, he had resorted to writhing and squirming uncomfortably over their low stone wall. Dressed, much like any young boy, in his usual faded blue jeans and a grey tee shirt, with some inane logo or other on the front, and wearing typical well-scuffed boys' trainers, he seemed be trying his absolute best to meld completely with the grey stonework of the wall itself. So completely eclipsed was he by the lavish and unending outpourings of attention being heaped upon his sisters that he seemed to have become bereft of any sense of personal worth of his own and, in his bewilderment, resorted now to wriggling about in painful silence as though he were the lowliest of creatures, if only to convince himself that he was still actually alive.

Then suddenly, out of this painful state of existential oblivion, he noticed me approaching with cheerful Sam by my side and the sheer relief upon his face could not have been more obvious. Immediately he leapt into action and in one great bound he was upon us. Fussing absent-mindedly over the dog while fixing his eyes on mine, he began to fire questions directly at me; *any* old question, *ludicrous* questions, it didn't matter what, all completely random and each one fired off even before I had a chance to answer the previous one. In the midst of this torrent I did just manage approvingly to acknowledge the girls and their mother but, with me already crouching down to his level, and with him strategically interposed between me and his sisters, he was able to impress himself upon me and to hold my attention prisoner for a good five minutes or more until my thighs began to ache and I had to stand up again.

The matter of sorting our children into their respective genders takes place very subtly and very gradually and, for the most part, unconsciously. So young Anthony's mother can have had no idea as to the depth of the discomfort she had caused him. She was simply doing much as any mother might do with her girls, helping them to *look* good to others so that they might be adored for their appearance. Supposedly, that is what girls are meant to be.

As for their brother, well... he was just a *boy*, wasn't he, doing what boys *do* and just being expected to get on with it! Boys, it seems, are not supposed to be adorable or fussed over for their appearance, let alone for their rosy sweetness and their blushing sensitivity. Boys, if they want to be noticed, cannot get by with just looking like boys; they have to behave like boys as well, they have to *do* things – be they good or bad – and the more they can do and the more impressively they can do it, the more likely they are to become noticed and, who knows, perhaps admired... even adored by others.

As a sequel to this, I was slightly surprised by what happened to me a short while later. I attended a conference in Cambridge on men and masculinity and, while I was there, I stopped over for a couple of nights with friends, notable academics and with two young sons, both gentle and good-natured souls and both of them like their parents, astonishingly bright and talented.

After the conference and back at my friends' house, we inevitably fell into a discussion in which several of those present just happened to be well-known authorities on gender issues. After a while my friend's youngest son, aged about ten, suddenly announced that he really wished he was a girl. When questioned why he responded that the boys at school were all so horrible, so competitive, so physical, domineering, unfeeling and so on.

Everyone present – mostly women – nodded thoughtfully and sympathetically and seemed to understand his point. And yet not one person present thought to question his assumption that, in order to be different, i.e. in order to become more gentle, thoughtful, considerate, sensitive, and so on, it was actually necessary for him to change his sex and become *a girl.*

To return to my point; so subtle and unconscious are the processes of gendering our children and separating them out into their opposite worlds that no-one present even assumed that a child might be all of these things... and more, perhaps, and yet still remain just an ordinary boy.

11

Spin Cycle

I think it is time now, my son, that you knew some more about your father. He was a good man and far cleverer than his critics would nowadays have us believe. Had you not fallen out with him, I am sure you would have come to the same conclusions as me. But that is another matter. He was named Kriek after his own father, your grandfather, who died in the wars against Histra before you were born.

As you now know, your father invented the automatic washing machine when he was still quite a young man, though you will also remember that he never made any money out of it. The sad truth is that he was never good at business and he neglected to take out the patent on his invention quickly enough. The company he worked for was owned, and still is in fact, by Baar-An and he quickly seized the chance and registered your father's invention in his own name, growing very rich on the profits, thank you very much!

Your father got no thanks or recognition and continued to work for Baar-An for the same low wages while watching him getting richer and richer on the fruits of his labours. In fact, not only did his employer never acknowledge your father's contribution to his fortune, he actually treated him very badly, so much so that his health eventually began to suffer.

But this was only the beginning. Now, although he had no head for business, your father was nonetheless an extremely clever and resourceful man and he kept on working on his invention in his own time, in his workshop at home, trying to improve on it so that one day he might be able to make his own fortune.

To begin with the improvements he made were not especially ground-breaking, although he did develop the front-loading machine with a glass door which made it much easier to load and unload. And the fact that you could also see clearly what was happening to your washing inside was, I thought, a brilliant idea. But, at the end of the day, it was still an automatic washing machine and he ran the risk of being accused of copying and exploiting the invention that his employer now claimed for himself.

The real break-through came sometime later, although by then your father's health was beginning to fail him. He was trying to develop a faster, quieter and more intelligent machine with a spin cycle so fast that it would get the washing much drier than conventional washing machines. In order to achieve this it had to be made robust enough to withstand the extreme forces involved, while keeping it light enough and small enough not to become cumbersome and unsightly. His work was progressing well when one day, while he was testing his new machine at high speeds, he noticed something extremely odd.

Apparently, when the advanced spin cycle reached a certain speed, certain items began inexplicably to appear in the wash, as if from nowhere. This was perplexing, as you can imagine, and at first he doubted himself. It took him a while to work out the precise speed at which this occurred, and the exact amount of time required, but sure enough, once he worked it out and repeated his tests, the results were consistent; certain items – to be exact, *socks* – began magically to appear in our machine as if from nowhere… nothing else, just socks, lots of them, and always odd socks, socks that were certainly never put there by us and so many, in fact, that we began to wonder what on Areth we were meant to do with them all.

Your father and I puzzled over these problems for ages, I can tell you. We talked and we talked until our throats were dry and our heads ached, but we got no further. It just didn't make any sense at all.

'But things don't just appear out of nowhere,' he would say to me in his frustration. 'And anyway... *why only socks?* Why not... *tee shirts...* or *underpants?'* And, for that matter, why were they never in pairs? Why did we only ever receive *single socks?* At least *pairs* of socks might have been useful!

We thought we would go mad trying to work out what was happening but then, one evening, your father had an idea. He immediately went back to his workshop to do some more tests, and he worked right through the night. Then, when he reappeared in the morning, he was smiling.

'I have found it,' he said. 'I know what's happening. I just don't know why yet.'

It so happens that, alongside his experiments on the advanced spin cycle, he had also been working on improvements to the rinse and filtration systems in the hope that he could separate out annoying tissue debris from the rest of the wash. Imagine that; no more irritating fragments of old tissue caught up in your clean clothes! Well, it seems that these socks only ever appeared at those times when he put tissues in with the washing to test out this new system. And, sure enough, every time he put tissues in with the wash, the tissues would completely disappear and, in their place, socks would appear. Tissues would go in, they would disappear completely, and then back came socks. And when he started to leave the tissues out of the wash altogether, guess what? *No socks!!*

You were still quite young then and I can tell you now that we racked our brains trying to make sense of it all but we .

got nowhere. We were well and truly stuck until finally your father decided to confide in someone else about his work and the strange results that he was getting. He had an old school-friend who worked at the university, someone who would listen to what he had to say. And listen he did. He was sceptical at first, understandably I suppose, but once he saw the machine at work he immediately took the problem to his head of department at the university, Hor-Kin, and, to our amazement, he became extremely excited. The three of them immediately entered into detailed discussions and at last it seemed that we might be getting somewhere.

Before long they found the funding to develop a research project to try to find out what exactly was going on. The formula seemed straightforward enough: S (speed) + T (time) + T1 (tissues) produced $\geq$ 1S1 (socks) and it was put rigorously to the test until, when no other explanation could be found, the team were forced to conclude the unthinkable; taking as given the fact that matter can neither be created nor destroyed, they were forced to accept that these could not be spontaneous appearances and disappearances because such thing ought never to happen. So they had to be either transmutations of matter or, more likely, exchanges of matter. And, if so, these phenomena had to be occurring somehow across space-time. It was the only explanation. Without realising it, your father had finally made an important breakthrough into the mysteries of space-time itself, with the added possibility that first contact may actually have been made with intelligent life from some other planet or parallel universe.

Immediately your father was given a full-time position at the university heading up a research team of his own and with the aim of tackling the mystery and developing his invention further. As improbable as it sounded, it was now almost undeniable that the improved version of the automatic washing machine that he had invented was serving as a portal, providing access to some kind of mysterious 'wormhole' in space-time. Physicists had long since concluded that space was actually curved, raising at least the theoretical possibility that, if some way could be found of travelling directly across this curve, through some kind of *wormhole* perhaps, then vast distances might be covered in hardly any time at all. It might even be possible to travel through time. But up to that point wormholes had remained just that; no more than a theoretical possibility with no practical means of ever discovering one, let alone accessing one and putting its practical uses for space travel to the test. It was your father, *your father*, who broke this impasse and he soon became famous as the one who finally turned this theoretical possibility into practical reality. This caused a huge amount of excitement, as you can imagine. So far, then, so good!

But while astrophysicists are extremely clever people – some might say a breed unto themselves – the public mind can be very fickle and the media barons are not best known for their intelligence or their open-mindedness. So when stories began to circulate about the invention of a portal to a wormhole, through which actual physical items could come and go through space-time, the press had a field day, making up wild stories and claiming – without any justification whatsoever – that contact really had been made with other intelligent life forms.

That was just the start of it; when the actual details of your father's work began to leak out it triggered a veritable bonanza for half-wits and loonies everywhere. Already the stories of contact with extra-terrestrials from some as-yet unknown region of the universe had whetted their insatiable appetites, but when it became known that the portal that provided the actual access to this wormhole was nothing more exotic than an automatic washing machine, the public went absolutely wild, even conducting their own ludicrous experiments. Stories began to circulate about people putting their pet hamstras, and even their poor *cats*, into their washing machines, only for them to perish horribly during the process.

In order to allay the hysteria therefore, your father's team had to assure the public that, so far, only paper tissues and odd socks had succeeded in travelling through the wormhole – if wormhole it was – and that inter-galactic space travel involving actual living beings was still a long way from possible.

Well, this backfired horribly. So palpable was the public disappointment that the media began to lampoon your father mercilessly, coming to all kinds of silly conclusions and suppositions of their own about just who these supposed extra-terrestrials might be.

Soon, wild conspiracy theories began to emerge claiming that this was all an elaborate plot to cover up the fact that top-secret deals had been made with aliens from another galaxy. And then crazy stories sprung up around some ongoing inter-galactic trade involving paper tissues and single socks, triggering preposterous tales of a race of supposedly one-legged extra-terrestrials who were forced, they deduced, to hop about from place to place like one-legged kangararas and who – as if that wasn't preposterous enough – appeared to suffer from constant colds and flu in the bargain!

Well, you can imagine… soon your father's reputation, as well as that of the university, began to suffer and, before long, funding for the project began to dry up. Your father's health got much worse until eventually he became unable to work. Then, to add insult to injury, after the project was dropped, his one-time employer, Baar-An, took over the development of the front-loading washing machine for himself and registered the patent in his own name. Your father died soon afterwards, a broken man.

And so, with the help of Baar-An and your father's advanced automatic washing machine, the continuing exchange of old tissues for odd socks has continued unabated, causing huge amusement for some, not to mention a certain amount of frustration, while the public's interest in wormholes and inter-galactic travel has waned almost to a whimper.

Yet even now, apparently, there are people who just cannot resist writing inane messages on their tissues before putting them into the machine. And of course, there are those of us as well who really don't mind wearing odd socks and who are therefore quite contented with the outcome.

Mind you, I do still wonder where they come from – all those odd socks – and who they really belong to. I mean, do they *really* only have one leg? That seems very odd to me!

Anyway, whoever they are, they are either very generous or very careless... and why on Areth would they want all our old tissues? That makes no sense to me at all!

12

Leap Year

Mary opened her eyes but remained quite still with her head lying heavy on her pillow. She had lain there like this for a while, eyes softly closed, warm and cosy, just timelessly day-dreaming. It was so comfy like this, so lovely and warm, so cosy. She didn't bother to look at the clock; she knew more or less what time it was by the light. And she knew what day it was only too well.

Today the early morning sun shone through the venetian blinds like a miracle, creating a bright ladder of light upon the white wall to her left; a ladder to Heaven. Just perfect! And somehow the longer she looked at it the more wonderful it seemed as she continued to lie there, still and happy, in her wandering day-dreams.

February 29th... a leap year. It was miraculous, to be sure. Somehow, in His infinite wonder, God had arranged that the Earth should travel round the sun just once a year and that every time it did so it should take *exactly* a year – no more, no less – to complete its journey. Truly amazing! How incredibly precise He was! And then – even more incredible – He should add on just one more day every fourth year... though she wasn't exactly sure why He should want to do this. Perhaps He just wanted to add a bit of variety to our lives. But it was not for her to question the mind of God. How wonderful He was! Always so very thoughtful!

As she lay there, warm and still, she continued to gaze at

her ladder of light while her mind drifted this way and that until it eventually took her back to her girlhood days at the Convent of the Sisters of Infinite Mercy, so many miles from Knocknacree where, according to her records, she had been born. They were not happy days. They were cold, austere and cheerless days, and all her childhood memories were overshadowed by painful flashbacks of her constant chastisement by the nuns. Beatings and the withdrawal of their awful food seemed now like almost daily occurrences and, on one occasion, when Sister Theresa had found her exploring herself in the bathroom, she was punished so severely that she had to spend several days recovering in the infirmary. There, cold and lonely but at least safe from the beatings, she dwelt on the Sisters' icy warnings that this was just a foretaste of the Hell that surely awaited her.

But that was then, and today the sun shone brightly just for her. Today would be sunny and warm, even though they were still in the grip of a long winter and spring's welcome release lay some way off. But in her heart it was spring, for sure. She was in love with the most wonderful man in the world and all the miseries and the pain of her bleak childhood melted away to nothing with this perfect thought.

She hugged herself tightly in her warm bed and wriggled a little with sheer delight at the thought of him smiling lovingly back at her. In her mind she heard him speak her name in his soft, gentle, yet confident voice, and she could see his warm, friendly smile in front of her, the kindness in his eyes and the way his hair shone gold when the light of the window was behind him. He was just perfect. She loved him more than words could say, and he loved her. And today he would be hers. She would pop the question and Heaven would be theirs at last.

She knew exactly what she was going to say, she had planned it for weeks. She had pictured the scenario in every detail and had memorised the words over and over in her head like a favourite record. He would be sitting there in his favourite chair, as he always did, the window just behind him and to his left, and she would be sitting where she always sat, slightly to his left so as not to be dazzled by the light from the window. Sometimes, when they sat like this early in the day, often saying very little, the sun would shine behind him like a halo round his head and the love would pour out of her like honey, like liquid gold.

Today she would start with the mention of his name, *Roger*. A wonderful name and she shivered at the very thought of him. Using his name like this would arrest his attention and he would look directly back at her, slightly quizzically perhaps, with those bright hazel eyes, curious, wondering what it was that his love wanted to say to him. And she would return his gaze like this for three, maybe four seconds – no more as this might make him feel uncomfortable – and then she would speak to him, softly, gently, loving and caring as she held his beating heart in her hands like a tiny fledgling bird.

'How long have we known each other now Roger?' she would continue, *'Two and a half... three years?'*

She knew exactly how long it had been; two years, nine months and eleven days since she arrived here on that mid-May morning, miserable and frightened, with the rain lashing at her face like nuns' tongues and with not so much as a shawl to protect her. Resting over the weekend, it would be another three days until she first laid eyes on him.

'You've had a very difficult time!' he said to her then and she nodded back nervously, not knowing what to say. She could not have known then that this man, this wonderful, lovely man, would one day take her to be his wife.

'You must know by now how I feel about you,' she would go on to say, *'and I know you feel just the same about me.'*

'Dear Roger,' she would continue, poised and ready to pop the question...

Just then, Mary was wrenched out of her daydream by two soft knocks at the door; two gentle knocks that did not ask to come in but announced instead that her door was about to be unlocked and opened. And when smiling Nurse Brophy walked in and looked at her, still abed and tousled with sleep, she chirruped:

'Would you look at you, Mary Hanlon, still in bed at this hour!' and as she spoke she lifted up her fob watch from the front of her white tunic, more as a gesture of confirmation than out of any need.

'Come along now, will you. You'll be missing your breakfast.'

Nurse Brophy, with her usual friendly demeanour and Exocet determination, saw Mary up and about in a trice and made sure that she had taken her first lot of medicines for the day. Before she went she took a moment to change the dressings on her left arm.

'Now come along and get your breakfast or that young Peter Maher will eat the lot!' Peter Maher, a full twenty stone and not yet in his twentieth year, could put it away like a mechanical digger.

At 11.07 that morning, according to her fob watch, Nurse Brophy found Orla Murphy, one of their older patients, waiting anxiously outside Doctor Breen's door and obviously late for her 11.00 appointment. The brass plaque on his door read, Dr. Roger Breen MD; FRCPsych, and below that the tab had been moved across to read, 'ENGAGED'.

'Oh dear me, is the doctor running late now!' the nurse

exclaimed and angled her left ear towards the door. She knocked lightly twice, with the back of two knuckles and then, when no reply came, she did so again and called out softly, *'Dr. Breen. May I come in?'*

As soon as she eased open the door she could see the Doctor slumped in his chair, covered with blood and with a pair of scissors protruding from the left side of his neck.

'Oh Jesus! Oh Mother of God!!!!' she cried out and as she rushed in to help him she caught sight of young Mary in the shadows to her right. She was sitting on the floor in the far corner, her knees up to her chin, huddled and rocking herself gently back and forth. And as she did so she seemed to be singing something almost inaudible to herself:

'And still she cries... I love him the best... and a troubled mind... surely knows no rest,'

Immediately the nurse slapped the large red emergency button on the wall behind the doctor and went to his aid:

'Doctor Breen, Doctor BREEN!'

'IN HERE! SOMEBODY HELP ME!' She shouted towards the door, half-drowned-out by the alarm bells jangling loudly outside in the corridor.

'God help us Mary, what have you DONE!!!'

Mary, at the far end of a trail of bloody footprints and spattered all over with blood, continued to rock in the corner while singing softly to herself:

'and still she cries... bonny boys are few... and if my love leaves me... what will I do?'

(Song: I Know My Love. Trad. Irish)

13

The Photograph

As a young boy growing up in London just after the war so many of the luxuries that we regard as perfectly normal today were simply un-dreamed of. Our 'everyday stuff' amounted to a cold, damp and draughty basement that we huddled together in, something we took to be a simple fact of life so we imagined nothing better.

We didn't exactly like it of course, but somehow we ceased to notice the mice and the smelly black mould, the lack of running hot water and the cold, because these were things we just took for granted. Our only heating was a paraffin stove, which we referred to affectionately as the 'glug-glug' on account of the noise it made, and a meagre coal fire in the sitting room which was only lit on the coldest of nights. Chill blains, something we never hear of these days, were just normal, something you just got. Such basic conditions, along with all the frugality and the rationing of the times, meant that ill-health was an almost constant feature of our lives.

Beyond the front door, the poor air quality was certainly a contributing factor to our health problems and, at its worst, London's famous yellow and sulphurous 'pea-souper' smogs must have been, for some, like a flashback to the terror of the trenches as they descended upon us, euthanizing the elderly and the most vulnerable without distinction or mercy. In my case, being officially *'delicate'* and suffering from chronic broncho-pneumonia, I was especially at risk. So it was with some irony that the peculiarly British enthusiasm for the 'fresh air cure' was administered to me with such ill-considered exuberance.

First there were the windswept convalescent homes, far away by the sea, and then the open-air special school by the banks of the River Thames where the estuarine fog conceded only to the bitter east wind as it whistled up from the North Sea like a banshee, hitting us full in the face and threatening to do for us all. Yet still, somehow, and miraculously, I survived all this and plenty more.

It was fortunate, then, that meeting one's end by getting run over was much less of a danger for us then than now. In those days to see a car at all in our street was almost a rarity, while essentials such as milk, sacks of coal, kegs of beer and such like, were delivered more sedately by means of horse and cart. The clip-clopping of hooves, the snorting, the horse-shit and the smells are all sensory delights that will remain with me forever. And, as regular as the deliveries, came the limbless war veterans who daily picked their way past our house with their tied up empty sleeves and trouser legs, still wearing their berets and medals proudly. Others, mustering what dignity they could, begged with set faces on the corners along the North End Road, each one of them fanning the flames of my young imagination; each one to this day an unopened story book.

And of course we played the long day as children do. There were a couple of playgrounds for young children within easy reach but mostly the car-less street was our theatre of choice. Here our play was entirely spontaneous, serendipitous and free of all adult contrivance, oozing out of our fertile imaginations like a fountain of dreams suddenly made real. Assorted pre-fabricated goodies and baddies such as cowboys and indians, English and Germans, cops and robbers, all guided the meandering paths of our plots and our wild-water narratives, while heroes such as Tarzan, Roy Rogers and Superman were prime roles to be fought over at the start of play.

Then, as we got a little older and more adventurous, there were the numerous bomb-sites, still un-cleared and just longing to be played on and explored. These became our instant cowboy 'Badlands' or perilous mountain ranges and during the summer we would catch various coloured butterflies and moths with our swishing fishing nets as they lingered over the thick clumps of bright yellow, wet-the-bed weeds. And as we reassembled the rubble into our various encampments and secret dens, there was always the lingering thrill of things to be found; treasures such as mangled fork or a crushed tin pot might eventually find their way to the rag and bone man, and might even help to earn us a dejected-looking goldfish in a polythene bag.

But among all our finds, the one that stands out, head and shoulders above all the rest, was that black and white photograph. Uncovered by Robert, one of the slightly bigger boys, he gasped and hooted, clutching it as close as he could to his chest and then holding it up and gawking at it over and over again and wailing with mixed disbelief and delight while the rest of us crowded in, desperately straining our necks and pleading for a look at his mysterious find. Once we realised what it was there would be no more play that day for there was simply no more useful imagination to be had. Scurrying back to the security of the street we packed around him excitedly all the way while he clung to his prize like a drowning man to a twig, the King of the Boys.

Much of the rest of the day was punctuated with outbreaks of hushed and excited conversation in small, spontaneous huddles, well away from parents and younger siblings who would surely blow the lid off the whole thing.

At school the next day the photograph surfaced again and, as soon as the playtime bell went, we were upon Robert like wasps, pleading once more and arguing about what should be done with the prize – for this was an object as much of fear and of dread as of mystery and forbidden delight – and surely, we reasoned, too much responsibility for one boy on his own.

In a quieter corner of the playground, where we would not arouse too much unwelcome attention, we all at last got a good look at the woman in the photograph. In black and white and subtler shades of yellowing grey, and naked from head to toe, she stood upright, looking back at us full on and blankly like any undressed shop-window dummy might. Her dark hair assembled into neat ringlets and curls, cascaded around her ears, framing an expressionless face that eschewed any possible hint of any kind of engagement, while the actual physical details of our dark and clandestine boyhood imaginings became fully de-mythed and revealed to us. From her slender neck to her neat round shoulders, to her bun-like, milk-white breasts with their large dark round nipples that seemed to glare accusingly straight back at us, to the strange curve of her hips and the shady well of her navel and, finally, the mysterious and darkly shocking, yet featureless expanse of her wide black pubic triangle… all left us gasping and our heads reeling.

A while later, having dispensed with the uninspiring realities of school dinner, we began to discuss what ought to be done with the prize. All enthusiastically agreed, apart from the finder of course, that such an image was far too precious and far too risky a thing to be retained by just one person. So, after much arguing and re-shuffling of rank, it was decided to dismember it and share out the details as carefully as possible so that we could all keep hold of some tiny part at least of its forbidden delights.

Painstakingly our friend began to tear the photograph, slowly and surgically, into neat monochrome rectangles and squares so that each boy would get his piece according to his status in the group. There were protests of course, amid some spirited argument and flexing of muscle. The smaller boy who was persuaded grudgingly to accept the head and face lived, he protested, in a houseful of framed photographs of women's heads and faces, so where was the thrill in that! To me, and surprisingly early in the pecking order, came a shoulder, her left one. Round and neat it had a kind of haunting perfection about it and I clutched it to my chest like a found banknote.

While the various parts of the photograph were distributed, piece by piece, among our individual members, we became magically transformed into *Our Gang* in the most esoteric sense of that term. Now we were special indeed. We had our very own sacred tokens of membership, easily worthy of any spy story, which could be matched up against each other and even reassembled, providing scope for further examination, as well as a deep sense of our closed and binding solidarity with one another, a sacred testimony of our hallowed belonging to what had suddenly become our very own, very secret society.

All the way home from school that afternoon my solitary piece of the photograph burned like a cinder in my pocket. I hurried back as fast as I could, convinced that people were looking at me and would just know my secret somehow, in that way that adults always did:

'That boy's got a naked woman in his pocket!'... *'Dirty little child!'*... *'Wait till I tell his mother!'*, so that by the time I arrived home I was almost in tears from the sheer effort of trying to maintain a straight and guilt-free expression. At home I headed immediately for my bedroom where I secreted

it at the bottom of a cardboard box, full of other valuable boyhood collectibles, which I then pushed far under my bed and where it remained hidden in the dark and the dust, as big as the bogey man, waiting for a quiet moment when I might just feel safe enough to feast my guilty eyes upon it once more. And there it remained, out of sight but seldom out of mind. At first the dread of being caught with it grew by the day while the actual image of the naked woman slowly faded from my mind's eye. Nobody ever discovered my secret and nobody read the story in my face.

In truth, of course, it could have been any old fragment of any old photograph, a knee perhaps, or even a large goitre for all the detail it provided, and no-one could have been any the wiser to my dark secret from this alone. Yet still, for a long time afterwards, weeks perhaps, the gremlin in my head haunted me, taunted me, tantalised me and tortured me in ways far worse than even the Brothers Grimm could ever have imagined, and I simply dared not venture back into the box again.

But time moves on quickly for young children and sometime later, when playing quietly in my bedroom, I did eventually retrieve my fragment of photograph for another look but it had mysteriously changed. Half-disappointed and half-relieved, I was surprised to find that I no longer recognised it for what it had once been. The object of all that dark fascination and excitement, along with its crippling payload of worry, all the shame and all the guilt, had simply faded back down to what it always had been; nothing more than a tiny snippet of insignificant grey paper set alight by the ever-hungry flame of a young boy's imagination.

14

Walter Fisher's Gate

Young Walter Fisher made his first gate when he was just twenty years old. It wasn't a full-sized, five-bar affair but comfortably big enough for one man and his dog, and he cut and planed the timber by hand and put it together almost as good as any trained joiner. These skills he had learned – just as he learned everything else –from his father, Walter Senior. He, his wife and Young Walter farmed a small piece of land not far from Saint's Green, near the Hertfordshire-Essex border. It was truly beautiful countryside, especially now in early summer, and so peaceful you could be a hundred miles from anywhere.

Once the gate was finished, father and son set off to fit it down near the bottom end of the East Field, not far from where the narrow track meets the main road to Falbury. It was a fine and sunny morning and, almost as soon as they arrived, Walter Senior headed back to the farm with the handcart, leaving Young Walter to hang it on his own and attach the furniture.

There was something immensely pleasing about making and hanging a gate, something about the way that it closed so snugly, no horrible creaks or rattles, only a satisfying metallic *clack* as the striker engaged and then shut fast.

An hour after he arrived, and happy with his work, Walter gathered together his few tools and put them into his loose jute bag, ready to head back home. As he went to pick it up he became aware of a crow whirling around overhead and making the most almighty racket.

'If that be a rook, that be a *crow!*' his father had said once and Walter recalled his little snippets of country wisdom as he stepped back through his new gate, closed it, and turned right towards the farm. Ten minutes should do it.

He had gone no more than a dozen paces when Lizzie Farr appeared at his side like a shadow, as if from nowhere.

'Been busy then, Young Walter?' she ventured, entirely unnecessarily as she had been watching him for the past ten minutes.

'Yup,' he answered. 'Been hanging that gate.' And he nodded towards his completed job with more than a tinge of pride.

'Made it myself too.'

Lizzie looked at him admiringly.

'I'm going to the store to get some flour for my mum,' she said. 'She'll be making bread. Want to come?'

Young Walter was still looking back at his handiwork and pretended not to hear.

'Want a look?' he ventured.

Lizzie eagerly accepted his invitation and Walter spent the next ten minutes explaining to her the intricacies of joinery and the hanging of gates. She didn't care that she was late or that her mother would chastise her for delaying the bread-making; she was in love and they don't have clocks there.

Walter too felt an unfamiliar pang and he became strangely aware of her closeness, the curves and the warmth of her body, and her frequent eye contact as she searched deeply into his own. There was no denying she was a pretty girl, a year or so younger than himself, with curly, shoulder-length black hair, tied back in a bow, and mischievous brown eyes. What really captivated him, though – now that she was standing so close – was her skin. Her face, only inches from his own, looked as soft and smooth as cream, faintly-tinged around her cheeks with the slightest hint of raspberry, and just a freckle or two around her nose. He might have reached out and touched her face right there and then, had his hands not been so conveniently splintered and grubby.

'Will you walk with me a way?' Lizzie suddenly asked, with one penetrating look that melted away any possible hint of shyness or resistance. As she did so she took one beckoning step back, her face still angled towards his, her eyes wide, smiling, inviting.

'Er… it'll take me a bit longer but… Yuh… *Yuh!*'

Walter's obvious timorousness made Lizzie feel all the more confident as she led him slowly back along the path and away from the farm like an obedient pony.

When Walter arrived back home, quite a bit later than expected, nothing was said. A long row of clean washing waved about in the breeze like a welcoming party, while his father looked up from what he was doing and acknowledged his return. Young Walter tried his hardest to look perfectly normal, as though nothing whatsoever had happened, but he found it difficult to concentrate. Years later his mother said that she knew all along.

Three weeks later Archduke Franz Ferdinand was assassinated and two months later, just before the harvest festival, war was declared. By that time Young Walter and Lizzie were said to be walking out together. They were blissfully happy and, over the coming months, they fell deeply in love, just as the dark and angry clouds gathered over Europe.

15

The Skip

There was a large skip half blocking the drive when he arrived; a huge, battered yellow-and-rust eyesore, stacked high with builders' waste and general neighbourhood detritus. It wasn't there three weeks ago when he last came to see her.

Today, though, was going be somewhat different. Wearing grey track suit bottoms and a blokey-black tee shirt, he strolled up to the front door, a little nervously, and rang the bell. As he did so he took a brief backward glance at the skip and the street beyond. The cherry trees were out in their thick pink blossom at last and a rather small young woman walked past, walking a huge dog that she might just as easily have ridden.

Almost immediately David was aware of footsteps approaching and he turned back to the door to see a dark, exploded shape through the large frosted, stained-glass panel. The latch was turned, the door pulled open, and there stood Melissa looking amazing, just like before, in that very understated but stylish way that she seemed to effect so effortlessly and yet so well.

'Hiya' she said cheerfully, 'Come on in.' The smile that greeted him was as colourful and unaffected as her dress style as she took a long step back for him to enter. Even with the front door open the hallway seemed dark but straight ahead of him he could see into the kitchen at the far end which was bathed in bright sunlight and colour.

'Come through,' she said, and ushered him round to his

right and into her workshop at the front of the house. She didn't offer him coffee; she never took food or drink in there for fear of accidents.

'Well, today's the day,' she beamed. 'How are you feeling?'

'OK,' he said, 'A bit nervous I suppose.'

'Of course,' she said. 'You'll be fine. Just hang your jacket over the back of that chair and we'll get started.'

The room was unusually large, getting on for eighteen feet square, and included a separate area curtained off in the far corner. Next to this stood a metal rail containing numerous items of clothing and his eyes instinctively scanned this for any familiar-looking pieces. Before getting started, Melissa sat down with him in the bay window area for a few minutes while she explained what had happened since they last met:

'I managed to get virtually everything,' she said, 'but I did have to make one or two adjustments. 'Did you manage to get the rest of what you needed?'

He had. Melissa's careful advice and recommendations had paid off well and he had managed to get everything he needed as well as some extras. As for shoes, he had found some slip-on sandals but they were a bit small and not especially attractive. At least he could make do with these until she came to the shops with him later in the week.

He felt very lucky that he had her to help him through this, someone so kind-hearted, so level-headed and helpful. It would all have been really difficult without her. As an experienced stylist and seamstress, Melissa had developed a particular skill for helping men who wanted to achieve that feminine look but without the bullock-in-ballet-shoes effect.

When David finally stepped out from behind the curtain, part of him felt a little self-conscious but, at the same time, he was really pleased with what Melissa had managed to achieve. The business of taking the plunge and dressing head-to-toe like a woman was never going to be easy, but the real difficulty lay in getting it right. So he had taken her advice very much to heart when they first met:

'Go easy,' she had said. 'What you don't want to end up with is Mr. Mutton dressed up as Miss Lamb!' So many men got this completely wrong, they agreed. Their frank conversations over the following weeks had been of enormous help as she listened with a supportive ear to what he had to say, while being gently matter-of-fact and always practical in the advice she offered.

She had worked with a number of clients like him before and, while each one was of course different, they all had one thing in common; a sense of being trapped, *'Held under water,'* as one client had put it. David knew exactly what they meant. For so long now he had felt obliged to live only a part of his life, keeping an entire side of himself hidden from view, never expressing how he really felt for fear of being ridiculed and rejected… yes, *fear!* Why was it that women had a license to wear whatever they pleased while, for doing no more than this, a man had to live with being labelled a cross-dresser or a transvestite – or even as sexually suspect – terms which were only ever applied to men, never to women.

Now, as he stood in front of the mirror and smoothed himself down, he felt himself relax into a smile and he noticed Melissa, over his right shoulder, smiling approvingly along with him. Still keeping one eye on her, he turned himself, first this way and then that, getting a better view of how he looked in the free-standing mirror behind him. And with each turn he became aware of how he would automatically rise up onto the big toe of each trailing foot and how, with each side-to-side movement his skirt would swish and flow softly around his

So anyway...

knees. These were new feelings, strange feelings, and oddly delightful. Somehow he felt much more aware of his body now, of how it moved and how it felt. He could never have explained why it felt so right; it just did.

'You look *great,*' said Melissa, still smiling as she took a step forward to check her work. 'It all fits perfectly.'

With a gentle tug here, and the slightest tweak there, she stepped back again and looked at his smiling face in the mirror. 'How does that feel? Are you pleased?'

'It feels great,' he replied and swished himself back round to face her. 'I'm amazed how well it all works. You've done a brilliant job.' For a brief second he felt quite tearful.

Of course he didn't have that female figure to set things alight, yet somehow Melissa had helped to choose and tailor an outfit for him that was both shapely and subtly stylish and which did not look at all pretentious or out-of-place on him. David had been reassured early on when she pointed out to him that not all women were especially shapely; lots had straight figures too and yet still managed to look good, so he ought to be able to do the same. At least he had a full head of hair which was already shoulder length and could be easily styled to fit the new look.

A further forty minutes or so was spent on the basics of make-up and the look was more-or-less complete. He studied himself in the mirror again before he left. Strange! What he saw was still unmistakably him, and yet an entirely different him. Then again, the new look was only part of the transformation; what really struck him was how it made him feel so different and he hadn't quite been prepared for this. Somehow this very same body felt unfamiliar to him now, and yet very comfortable and pleasant to be in.

As he got ready to leave he and Melissa made arrangements to meet on Thursday morning and, as he left the house, sporting a brand new shoulder bag containing the rest of his newly-acquired clothes, she watched him with interest as he walked with a certain poise back down the drive towards the street. As he did so, and without looking back, he casually tossed his holdall, containing the clothes he came in – especially that ludicrous 'Keep On Truckin' tee shirt – into the very centre of the skip.

And from there he stepped out very happily, if slightly warily into the street and a whole new adventure.

16

In the Picture

Doreen's life had taken a change for the better just recently. For a long time after Fred died she just didn't know what to do with herself. She had few real friends of her own to speak of, and nobody she knew well enough to talk to about her jumbled feelings.

It was a difficult time for sure. Fred wasn't an easy man to live with and always had to have his own way. And, true, he was never actually violent, but his moods were predictably unpredictable and his temper could, at times, be truly Krakatoan. Nor was he keen on Doreen having any kind of life of her own beyond him. So after he died three years ago, on the day before her sixty second birthday – and even though her life seemed quite empty and desolate at first – there was a part of her that was really quite glad to see the back of him. He was a tyrant and a bully; she could admit this to herself now.

Fortunately her son Edmund lived not too far away and he and his second wife, Jo, were as supportive as they could be. But Edmund travelled a lot with his work and Jo had a demanding job as a deputy headmistress and this meant that, after the dust settled, quality time with them became once again less frequent. On the plus side, this also meant that Doreen got to help out more regularly with their young daughter, Charlotte, who was five now and as bright as a button. She enjoyed this and didn't mind at all that it could be such hard work.

About a month ago, when Edmund and Jo had to go to a funeral in Edinburgh, Charlotte stopped over with Doreen for a couple of days and they spent long happy hours with paper and pencils and crayons and paints and pots of glue and coloured paper... and 'Silly Nana' went and got blue paint in her eye, which stung a lot, and Charlotte thought she was crying. But Doreen's days of crying were long-past.

That was around the time that she got to know Trevor. Being a near-neighbour, she knew him to say hello to but it wasn't until a large branch fell off a tree at the front of her house that they got to talking properly. He led the Gentle Walking Group at their local U3A and encouraged her to join and, since then, she had made several new friends, really nice people, and most of them, it appeared, rather passionate about wine, including Trevor.

Soon afterwards he took her to a wine bar in town where the wine and the conversation flowed free and Doreen ended up a little tipsy and loose-tongued. Since then they had grown quite close and now she found him almost constantly on her mind.

Tonight they were going to the theatre, their first actual date, and she was reminded of how it felt to be a young woman again; those little pangs of excitement inside that take off suddenly, like sparrows, just when your mind is on other things.

Doreen was sitting at the kitchen table, drinking her morning coffee and having second thoughts about her dress, when the post arrived. In among the usual letters and circulars was a largish brown envelope, stiff-backed, and addressed to Nana Doreen in blue felt-tip pen a-la-Charlotte.

Doreen opened this one first, and extra carefully, to reveal a brightly-coloured-in child's portrait of herself entitled 'nana' in large letters at the bottom. It was a delightful surprise and almost moved her to tears just to know that Charlotte was thinking of her. She noted too how she had suddenly moved on from those twig-limbed figures to people with multiple protruding chipolatas, each one coloured in differently. It was hilarious and wonderful. But who was the man that she had drawn in next to her in black crayon? It couldn't be Fred; she was too young to remember him properly and had never mentioned him before. And it certainly couldn't be Trevor because they had never met and, anyway, she knew nothing of him.

Still, she would be collecting Charlotte from school this afternoon and she could ask her then. So she put it to the back of her mind for the time being, finished off her coffee, and went back upstairs to make a final decision about that dress.

When she collected Charlotte that afternoon it was raining hard so they hurried home for drinks and chocolate biscuits and games and afternoon TV until Jo came to collect her after work. Such illicit treats were Nana's special privilege and much to be frowned-at, yet somehow all the more special for that.

In the sitting room, while Charlotte was sitting on the settee in front of the television, Doreen chose to ask her about the man in the drawing. To her astonishment, she took a brief sideways glance and replied:

'What man?'

'*This* man, Darling,' said Doreen, almost laughing. '*Here,* in your picture.'

'There isn't any man,' insisted Charlotte and turned back again to the animals on the television.

'This man *here!*' repeated Doreen, slightly flummoxed now.

'*Nana...*' said Charlotte, in her slow and most precocious voice, 'there *isn't* any man, just *YOU... LOOK!*' and she prodded Nana's triangle-and-chipolata image on the page several times with her finger as she spoke.

'Charlotte!' exclaimed Doreen, aghast, but her granddaughter had spoken and ignored any further insistences in favour of a delightful baby hippopotamus on the TV.

By the time Jo knocked at the door on her way home from school, Doreen was feeling hopelessly confused. She had got no more out of Charlotte and so, just as her mother was going out the door, she asked her to take a quick look at the picture as well. Grimacing in the rain she took a very quick backward glance and they were off.

Doreen stood there dumbfounded as she watched them scurry off towards the car, completely unable to believe what she had just heard:

'*No! No man, just you!*'

She was still standing at the open doorway as they drove off, still staring at the man in the picture, right there, unmistakable, in bold black crayon and as large as life.

By now she was beginning to feel quite distressed about the whole thing so she immediately called Trevor, but there was no answer. So she left him a message to call her back when he got a moment, and she waited... and she looked again at the picture... and she waited some more... until, eventually, the time came for her to start getting ready. But now she was feeling so anxious and in such a jitter that she managed to break a nail, and then ended up having to take off her makeup and do it all over again.

So by the time Trevor rang the front doorbell she was a mess of nerves. Releasing the latch, she called out to him:

'Hi. Just a moment,' and she checked one last time to see that she had everything she needed: keys, phone, money, lipstick, etc., and then she paused to check herself briefly in the hallway mirror before leaving the house.

Then she saw him. Standing immediately behind her and watching over her left shoulder stood Fred, as clear as day, looking straight back into the mirror at her, straight back into her eyes and at his most belligerent.

In shock, Doreen spun round and let out a loud scream and as she did so she slipped and fell, banging her head hard on the newel post before falling heavily onto the tiled floor.

Trevor called out and pushed open the front door, which was half obstructed now by Doreen's legs, one shoe off, to find her lying unconscious and bleeding from a gaping wound above her left eye.

His phone had stopped working earlier that day so, without hesitation, he reached into Doreen's bag for her phone in order to call the ambulance. As he did so, Charlotte's loosely folded drawing fell out of her bag and now lay open across Doreen's unconscious body; a triangular lady with straight grey hair and chipolata limbs, standing all on her own next to a row of colourful lollipop flowers.

17

Bob's Wife

Bob's wife could really talk… I mean *really* talk. There was no denying the fact. All of her friends said so and, even though they were fond of her, they also light-heartedly agreed that, once she got going, there was hardly any stopping her.

Many a Friday evening she would meet up, 'early-doors', with 'the Girls', as she called them, in one of several wine bars in town, thus both avoiding the hordes of late-night revelers while, at the same time, having a reasonable chance of getting seated together and being able to hear each other speak. Sometimes they would round off the evening with tapas or something else to eat.

And the more the wine flowed, the more Bob's wife would talk nineteen to the dozen about anything and everything, to the point where shy Marianne and one or two others would simply give up trying to get a word in edge-ways and so just carried on listening and laughing along with the others. And, in truth, nobody really minded that much because she could be so entertaining, giving free rein to a savage wit and a sense of humour that lay somewhere on the darker side of outrageous.

But, once in a while, Mrs. Bob, as one or two of them called her, didn't make it as her daughter from Southampton visited regularly. So it was not entirely unusual for the Girls to meet up amongst themselves and, of course, there would be times when she would come up in conversation. None of them actually knew very much about her, partly because no-one ever got a chance to ask, she being so garrulous and forward. Yet somewhere along the line they had picked up on the fact that she had been a school secretary at some point before she retired and that she lived with someone called Bob, presumably her husband.

So when, later on – and to the Girls' astonishment – they discovered that he too talked almost non-stop, they could hardly contain themselves.

'My Bob? Deary me, you should hear him!' she said one day over a cup of coffee. 'Never stops talking. Drives me completely potty sometimes!'

Quite by chance she had bumped into Marianne in town, just as she was coming out of the hairdresser's and, from there, with their heavy bags of shopping, they took themselves off to a nice little Italian caffe nearby where they chatted and where their conversation soon turned to life at home.

'No... just me and Bob,' she had replied to Marianne's question, 'No-one else. But, of course, our Linda comes to visit regularly as well and she's good company. Not like Bob!' she guffawed, rolling her eyes skywards as she spoke.

'Don't you get on?' asked Marianne, innocently and trying her best not to sound nosey. She was a quiet and good-natured woman who always saw the best in people.

Bob's wife looked back at her oddly for a second and then added, 'Well, he's not exactly good company is he... I mean he doesn't actually do anything! He just sits there. He does like the TV on a lot of the time and that seems to keep him happy, which is fine with me. I don't really watch it that much myself. But then he talks all the way through it anyway, non-stop, so I don't get to hear a bloomin' thing!' At this she laughed loudly above all the noisy chatter, having then to wipe the coffee off her chin as well as the table top.

Marianne looked back at her sympathetically, almost tragically.

'Really?'

'Absolutely,' she said, noting her expression… 'Mind you, don't 'get me wrong; I mean, I love him to bits but I do wish he'd shut up sometimes. He can be a right pain in the bum!'

When Marianne unintentionally divulged this deeply tantalising snippet of information to the Girls at the wine bar, it detonated sudden shrieks of such loud and raucous laughter that everyone else in the bar fell quiet for a moment. The irony of the situation was unavoidable and so glaring that it sparked off a whole string of pointed, even if well-meant jokes and comments and wild hypotheticals:

Jan, for example:

'If they both talk all the time, I mean… if neither of them ever shuts up, how on Earth do they manage to discuss anything at all?'

There was some shaking of heads among The giggling Girls.

'Maybe they have to put their hand up when they want to speak,' piped up, Laura, sparking off another burst of laughter.

'Or Perhaps,' responded Andrea, hardly able to speak at all for laughing, 'perhaps they've got a large conch shell that they pass between them, like in the *Lord of the Flies!*'

More loud hoots of uncontrollable laughter at the very idea.

'Then again,' suggested Laura as the laughter began to subside, 'maybe they just talk over each other so that nothing ever gets heard. What must it be like!'

'It must be *Hell!*' added Julie, and all agreed and laughed some more.

But then, as the laughter ran its course, all were left wondering,

what was it *really* like at home?

Did they ever come to blows in their desperate attempts to get a word in edge-ways?

Surely it must cause rows between them! It must do!

And what was Bob like?

The Girls looked curiously at one another. None of them actually knew. They hadn't even known Jane that long, only a few months really, since she retired and moved here from the other side of town. And, because she was always the one doing all the talking, they had actually found out very little about her.

They tried to picture the cacophony at home with all that constant talking, but no-one had ever been there so there was nothing to go on. That in itself became a point of further interest, adding to the now deepening mystery of Mrs. Bob's equally loquacious husband.

Then, for a couple of weeks, there was nothing. Ordinarily, if she couldn't make it one Friday, she would call Josie, or maybe Julie, but when one Friday passed without a word, and then another, the Girls began to become concerned. This wasn't like her at all.

In the end it was kindly Marianne who elected to call her the next day to check that she was OK. She had already made that first tentative contact anyway so it would sound less out-of-place if it came from her. With that the Girls ordered another bottle of white wine and some snacks and then went back to chatting amongst themselves.

On Saturday morning after breakfast Marianne and her husband Charlie walked the dog. It was wet, muddy and cheerless so when they got back, and having dried off Jasper, they were glad of a hot cup of tea and a sit-down with the paper.

But, before drinking her tea, Marianne called Bob's wife to see how she was.

Apparently she was fine but, for a while now, she had been having some trouble with a tooth which had then become infected. Finally it became too much and, on top of several painful trips to the dentist, she was given a course of antibiotics which seems to have done the job. But this also meant no alcohol. So, feeling miserable and unable even to drink, she turned up the heating and buried herself away with a couple of good books until it was all over.

'Look,' she said in the end, 'why don't you come round for a cup of coffee later. I could use a friendly face.'

Marianne, always supportive and willing to help, agreed to come round that afternoon with a special offer of pastries for the recovering patient.

'Can you eat pastries?'

'You just watch me!'

When she rang the doorbell at around 2.30 she brought with her not only a bag of pastries but also some flowers. She was a warm-hearted and good-natured woman and not beyond a pang or two of conscience for having had such a good old laugh at her friend's expense.

As Mrs. Bob answered the door she was drying her hands and was clearly delighted to see Marianne.

'Come on… come on in. Jeeeesus, is it *still* raining! Here, give me your coat… for *me?* Oh that's lovely, thank you so much. Oh aren't you kind, they smell gorgeous. Come on through to the kitchen and I can put these in water while the kettle's boiling. You must be frozen. You know, they were saying on the radio just now about this *'La Niña effect'* – come on through – you know, where all the cold water banks up in the Atlantic… or is it the Pacific? And they say that it's going to create a long, cold wet winter. Blimey, I'm not looking forward to that, I can tell you! La *bloomin' Niña…* can you *believe* it! As if we don't get enough cold wet weather as it is! Do you take sugar? Come on, come through to the sitting room. I'll put these in water later. You can say hello to Bob!

As though taking its cue from Mrs. Bob, the rain carried on almost non-stop for most of that week, though it did at least warm up little as Friday approached and as the wind eased its way round to the south west.

She was going to be fine. This week was half-term so her daughter from Southampton was bringing her granddaughter up to see her for a few days. Sadly, though, this also meant that she would miss yet another night out with the Girls. But still, at least Marianne could report back to them with the news that she was all OK.

But what to say about Bob! She wasn't at all sure how best to broach this one with the Girls. But as the week wore on, and their night out came round again, she resigned herself to the inevitable, got herself ready, checked that she had her bus pass, and set off for the wine bar, biting her lip for much of the way.

That evening she seemed a little subdued at first and didn't say very much. But once the Girls got settled in and then cottoned on that she seemed rather quiet, they asked her if she was alright. They were keen as well to know how Mrs. Bob was doing. Was she OK?

'Oh the poor thing!'

'Oh, How miserable!'

And then came the inevitable question:

'And did you meet Bob?'

The Girls fell quiet in anticipation of Marianne's response so, after a uncomfortable pause, they all caught the look on her face... how her cheeks flushed red as she hesitantly made to answer.

They simply couldn't help themselves; with one great shriek the noise levels erupted through the roof of the wine bar until the whole place stopped and stared at them, wondering what on earth was going on. A half-full bottle of wine had already been knocked over, causing a couple of the Girls to leap to their feet, while others choked on theirs and the rest – apart from poor Marianne – howled and reeled in their seats and clutched at their sides, or at each other's arms, and dabbed furiously at their eyes with tissues, sobbing with uncontrollable laughter.

It took an age for things to start to quieten down and, by then, most of those in the wine bar had given up on what they were doing and were now paying rapt attention to the group, eager to find out what all the noise and hilarity was about.

Eventually some of those sitting close by could just make out Andrea's half-stifled response to herself amid the continuing rumblings of laughter from her friends:

'Oh… I don't believe it!' she gasped, her voice rising hysterically in pitch as she struggled through her own laughter to get the words out.

'Oh my God!' she howled, even louder…

'Oh dear, dear me!' she sobbed, her face streaked with mascara tears.

Bent almost double in her chair now, her words and her breath failing her, she almost didn't make it and only just managed to splutter the words:

'A parrot! Oh dear, dear me! *A… BLOODY… PARROT!!!*' At which point she completely lost all control and wet herself laughing.

18

The Waterfall

Stanley sat quietly on his own by the edge of the stream while dipping his fishing net repeatedly but absent-mindedly into the water beneath the bank. This was one of his favourite pastimes and ordinarily he would be charged with excitement at the thought of catching something. Mostly this would be minnows, the males flashing blood-red and silver like butchers' knives at this time of year as they darted about in the fast-flowing water, this way and that, in search of love. Miss Davies had told him this at school only a week or so ago and for a moment it had rekindled his boyish zest for life. But his spirits soon sunk again under the weight of what had happened at home.

Once he had caught a gudgeon like this but they too lived on the bottom… and they too were hard to reach.

The minnows, however, were too alert and much too fast for him today and as his interest flagged he sat back down heavily on the bank and felt for the small biscuity snack in his pocket. As he did so his hand also settled on the letter and he withdrew them both at the same time, examining the folded piece of paper as he fumbled to unwrap the silver foil that contained his snack.

He knew what the letter said; he had read it over and over again and each time it churned his insides like a washing dolly, making him feel sick and angry, all in one big mess.

Why did it have to be like this!

Once upon a time things were fine. He was only little then and didn't remember that much but his mum and dad seemed to get on OK and Jill – his older sister by three years – well, she was just like all big sisters he imagined, bossy and superior.

But then there was the morning when his mother was making breakfast while nursing a black eye… purple and red actually, but it did look very painful. And she had been crying too. This worried Stanley a lot and he pleaded with her:

'What's wrong Mummy? What's the matter? What's wrong with your eye?

But she said that everything was fine and that he needed to eat his breakfast all up or he wouldn't grow into a *big* boy.

And then it happened again… and again, as the rows became louder, angrier and more frequent and even more frightening.

Time dragged on like this until one damp morning, about four weeks ago, when the police came to his house and took his father away and his mother had to go to the hospital to get her arm mended.

That was when the sadness started. It felt like a ginormous black blanket that descended on him, heavy and hot, as though one of their cows had sat on him, and it weighted him down and blocked out all of the light. He didn't want to eat and he didn't want to play and, although he went back to school after a day or two, it was like they were all strangers and he felt all alone, as if he was in a different place from them.

The envelope containing the letter was handed to him by his cousin, David, at school last week and when he read it at play time he cried.

It began:

Dear Stanley,

I am so sorry about what happend and Im realy sorry. I never wanted to hurt your mummy and I dident mean to but I became so angry and I dident know what else to do. It just came out of me like that and Im so sorry.

So I have decided to go away for a while. That is best for your mummy and it is best for me as well as I can hopfuly start a new life somewhere else.

I am not angry now but I am very sad because I miss you and I dont see you any more. But I hope I will see you again one day soon and I can take you out and we can do any thing you like. Prehaps we can go fishing together. Would you like that.

I am sorry if I made you sad and frigtend. I dident mean to. Honestly, and I will make it up to you. Promise.

Please dont show this letter to your mummy.

I will write to you again soon.

I love you very very much.

Daddy XX

Stanley read the letter again; it must have been for the hundredth time. Why didn't he want him to show it to his mother? He didn't understand. None of this made any sense to him and the more he thought about it the more sad and anxious it made him feel. He missed his father but somehow that only made him feel worse. All these feelings... it was all so confusing. He wished life wasn't so messy.

Without thinking he began to fold the piece of paper, in half first of all, then turning over the corners until, almost before he realised, he found himself cradling a small paper boat in his hands. The rest happened almost mechanically.

As he knelt down next to the river bank he placed a tiny

stone in the bottom for ballast and then, very gently, rested his paper boat on top of the water where it tilted a bit to one side and then slowly set off on its own downstream.

Less than ten yards further on Stanley watched it as it suddenly picked up speed and, a second or two later, launched itself over the top of the small waterfall, down and out of sight, along the river and on its way.

19

AbracaDeborah

Christmas Morning and Deborah was wide awake in a flash. Barely seven o'clock, still dark, rain spattered on the windows. But it wasn't so much the crisp rustle and the bulk of several mysterious objects against her feet that woke her so much as the sudden fizz of expectations that exploded like popped champagne in her head. Out of her deep, warm, cosy dreams of sweet little ponies and magical godmothers, she sat suddenly bolt upright as if on a spring, pulling her duvet down to her waist and reaching instinctively across for the lamp switch next to her bed.

In the bright light, and barely pausing for breath, she grabbed the nearest present to her and hurried out of bed and into her brother's bedroom next door.

'Anthony! *ANTHONY!*' she hissed in her loudest and most urgent whisper. 'Anthony! Look!' she insisted, shaking him vigorously. Her first present was unwrapped almost before he could open his eyes and she waggled a pretty matching scarf and woolly hat in front of his face.

'Look what I've got!'

Having woken him she immediately turned on her heels and was gone, hurrying back to her own bedroom in search of further delights.

It didn't take long before the excitement and the hullaballoo next door woke Mum and Dad, providing the untimely cue for an early morning cup of tea. And almost inevitably, with the first hint of movement from them, their room was immediately invaded by a squirm of noisy and excited bodies, quickly joined by that of Polly, their excited black Labradoodle. In barely two ticks of the clock the fun and festivities had begun. Christmas had burst in upon them like an oompah marching band and any thoughts of resistance, let alone peace and quiet, were immediately abandoned. Yielding to its driving rhythms the whole family followed Mum downstairs with bleary-eyed Dad shuffling along somewhere at the rear.

It was still far too early for breakfast proper so while Mum and Dad slowly came round, supping their cups of tea in comfy chairs, the children hurriedly spooned down their breakfast cereal amid bouts of excited chatter about their freshly-opened early presents. To their delight, the mince pie and the glass of brandy that had been left out for Santa the night before had gone and in return, beneath the winking Christmas tree, a large assortment of colourful and neatly-wrapped presents waited impatiently, like a stack of dynamite on a very short fuse.

But the main opening of presents was to happen later, once all the protests had died down and everyone was washed and dressed and breakfasted, and once all those little jobs were attended to, like washing up and drying and putting away and tidying round, and once Dad had taken Polly for a short walk round the block. Only then, only then could they all sit down together with a nice cup of coffee and an early mince pie and start to open the presents. And, of course, there were bound to be even more presents later when Grandma and Grandad arrived for Christmas dinner.

To the excited children all these preliminaries seemed to take an eternity but, eventually, the kettle went on and the mince pies were warmed and the family cosied into the sitting room and started, at long last, to unwrap their presents.

Sat cross-legged amid an expanding pile of wrapping paper and assorted packaging, Anthony's new games console caused great excitement, while Deborah's fancy new scooter had to be brought down from upstairs so as not to spoil the surprise. And there was so much more; presents and goodies and sweets and surprises galore! Mum and Dad, newly adorned in their Christmas socks and reindeer sweaters and glowing with contentment, joined in with the excitement as each new surprise burst forth, only to become quickly eclipsed by the next.

Finally the pace slowed and only one more present remained beneath the tree, a bit of a mystery actually since no-one had noticed it up until now. And although the card clearly said it was for Deborah – there was no mistaking that – there was no indication at all as to whom it was from. Certainly Mum and Dad had no idea; they couldn't even recognise the handwriting on the gift card.

So, while they all looked on with expectant faces, Deborah eagerly set about tearing off the wrapping paper to reveal a large, brightly-coloured box emblazoned with colourful pictures of her very best and most favourite heroes and, in large ornate letters on the top, the words:

HARRY POTTER – OFFICIAL WIZARD'S BOX.

'Oh *Wow!*' she exclaimed, looking wide-eyed into her parents' still querying faces. 'Harry Potter! Harry *Potter!*' Even though Hermione was her actual favourite this minor inaccuracy hardly registered at all.

Among the contents of the box she found a shiny black magic wand (surprisingly heavy) and a set of round Harry Potter glasses – plastic lenses of course – and a button-up black gown, plus an invisibility cloak – both neatly folded – a yellowing map of Hogwarts and a quite substantial-looking book of spells, and so much more besides.

For almost an hour, while the rest of the family got on with other things, she amused herself leaping around the house like a magpie on steroids, with her black gown flowing behind her, waving her wand and casting her magic spells this way and that, *'Haaah!'* here, and a *'Wuaaah!'* there, banishing evil and all nasty things from the land for evermore.

Once in a while, though, she would take time out to consult her book of spells, trying her very best to read and learn each incantation by heart, but needing her parents help in order to read them at all. Fortunately, for Polly the Dog, the doorbell rang just in time to prevent her from being transformed into a fluffy pink pony. Moments later Grandma and Grandad were all but dragged into the house by the excited children.

Yet more presents arrived with them and were soon opened and then there was even more tea, plus an early glass of whisky for Grandad, until at last the time came to tidy away any remaining wrapping paper and packaging, taking extra care to make sure all presents were accounted for first.

Then, while Mum and Dad, aided by Grandma, busied themselves with preparations for Christmas dinner in the kitchen, and while Anthony played with his games console in the dining room, Deborah and her Grandad amused themselves for a while reading spells and practicing magic to amaze the family with later on. Only, in truth, grandad wasn't especially enthusiastic about such things and all-too-soon lost interest.

So when Deborah's invisibility cloak failed to deliver on its initial promise, and even though she was clearly disappointed, Grandad – ever they cynic – was lost for what to say.

Finally he piped up:

'I can make you invisible.'

Deborah was immediately captivated, even if slightly suspicious. 'Can you! I mean, can you *really?'*

'Of course I can. It's easy. But you'll have to do exactly

what I say,' replied Grandad, sounding very knowledgeable now.

Deborah listened with rapt attention to his instructions.

'Right, first of all you need to go upstairs.'

'Upstairs?' she queried.

'Yes, right to the top, mind you. Let me know when you're on the landing.'

Deborah hurried upstairs getting increasingly excited by the ultimate promise of invisibility.

'OK. I'm upstairs now Grandad,' she called.

'Right at the top?'

'Yes,' she called back down.

'OK. Now, you have to turn around three times... but be careful not to fall down the stairs.'

'Three times?'

'Yes, that's it.'

Moments later she called back downstairs again. 'I've done that Grandad. Now what?'

'Right,' responded Grandad, 'now you need to hop three times, first on one foot and then the other.'

'Three times?'

'Yes,' he replied. 'Three times on each foot.'

There was some low-level thumping noise from the landing as Deborah carried out her grandad's instructions to the letter.

'Done it,' she called back down.

'Now,' said Grandad, 'what you need to do now is to close your eyes and blow really hard three times – three times mind you – otherwise it won't work.'

'Done that,' called Deborah excitedly from the top of the stairs.

'Good,' Grandad called back. 'Now you're invisible.'

There was a moment's pause, so loud that he could almost hear it from the sofa downstairs.

'No I'm not!' Deborah retorted, sounding a touch cross.

'Yes you are,' insisted Grandad.

'No I'm *not!* I'm *NOT!'* replied Deborah, obviously disappointed and getting increasingly cross.

'Well, I can't see you!' responded Grandad, trying his hardest to contain his laughter.

There was another pause… a little longer this time.

'That's because I'm *upstairs!'* protested Deborah, her hands on her hips and stamping her foot.

Grandad could contain his laughter no longer and when Deborah stomped back downstairs again she found him doubled up on the sofa almost crying with laughter. This made her even more cross.

Holding back her tears she stamped and shouted, 'You're very naughty Grandad! I don't like you!'

Soon enough delicious smells started to waft in from the kitchen, accompanied by the clattering sounds of increased activity as the first signs of Christmas dinner began to appear.

'Dinner everyone, *dinner's ready!'* came the call from Mum in the hallway.

Anthony was called from upstairs and told to wash his hands before coming down.

'Come on everyone, we don't want it getting cold.'

'Have you washed your hands? Good! Come on Anthony. Deborah, put that away now. You sit there Grandma.'

As the family assembled to take their places at the table, Dad began to serve up slices of turkey and trimmings amid approving noises and the shuffling of plates and spoons and dishes of food.

When Mum came through from the kitchen with the gravy there was still one empty place at the table.

'He'll be washing his hands,' said Grandma dismissively.

'He always takes ages.'

Mum found a space for the gravy and called upstairs, 'Grandad, dinner's on the table.'

'Grandad!'

When there was no response she went upstairs to check on him.

'Grandad,' she called out again, 'Grandad?'

She checked the bathroom and all the bedrooms.

'Grandad, where are you? Your dinner's getting cold!'

But he was nowhere to be found.

Downstairs again and frowning deeply, she called into the dining room, 'Has anyone seen Grandad?'

Everyone looked at each other with slightly concerned faces.

In their preoccupation, no-one noticed Deborah as she leaned forward and chose one particular sausage from the serving dish.

Sitting patiently beside her, Polly licked her lips and waited in quiet anticipation.

20

A Hot Night in June

The first time Paulo saw her he was captivated. She was quite simply the most beautiful woman he'd seen for a long time, and he had known quite a few.

It was hot for early June, almost too hot, and still relatively quiet, even here so close to the sea. The main influx of tourists would not arrive for another three weeks yet, so today, having no work and being a weekday, he planned on having the beach almost to himself. But first he had urgent need of a cool beer and headed towards a small shady *chiringuito*, off to one side of the track that led down to the beach. And there she sat, all on her own in the shade, sipping occasionally, and somewhat absent-mindedly, at a glass of white wine.

Hardly able to resist, Paulo placed himself at a nearby table where he could watch her, but without appearing to stare, and ordered himself a beer. She didn't seem to notice him or anything else much. The olives on the table next to her remained untouched while she read her book and scribbled occasional notes in the margins with a thin, pink plastic pencil. From some way behind her came the restless sounds of the sea and of small children playing happily while, between the trees, he could make out the island of Ons, stretched out full-length like a crocodile on the horizon, as though sunning itself.

She was too fair for these parts, possibly English or German, maybe French, but her skin tone said she was used to such sunny climes.

When he finally walked over and spoke to her, she lowered her book and looked up at him over the top of her sunglasses, with brown, inquisitive but confident eyes. And when he asked if he could join her, she responded in competent Spanish but with a distinct French accent and a certain huskiness in her voice that made her almost irresistible to him.

He sensed her interest in him; the way she looked at him, not the least bit put out by his interruption and possibly even pleasantly surprised. She even put her book and her pencil down and soon they were chatting away like friends, partly in Spanish and partly in broken English. Paulo knew no French.

Her name was Carla, and she was here for three months doing research on Celtic folklore. She was quite simply stunning, beautiful in that understated way that only edged her that much closer to the brink of perfection. And it made him want her all the more. It was like coming face-to-face with someone out of a fairy tale.

She liked him too, though she was distinctly cautious when it came to matters of the heart. Still, he was very handsome, tall and manly, giving off a kind of alpha-male animal attraction without being in any way brutish. His wide smile, his white even teeth... and those dark hungry eyes, all drew her to him like a magnet in spite of herself.

Instead of heading for the beach Paulo stayed with her in the shade and they talked and shared a bottle of wine and some tapas while they got to know one another. He wasn't from these parts, though she couldn't quite pin down where, but he was spending the summer inland, up in the hills a way, where wild horses roamed and where he eked out a living frugally while restoring an old granite house and barn.

'You must come and see where I live,' he said. 'It is very beautiful. I know you will like it.'

There was a slight tinge of hesitation in Carla's eyes and

in her voice. She was staying further up the coast, not far from Santiago and the University where her studies kept her extremely busy. She also travelled quite a lot, conducting interviews and other research for what would eventually be a book of her own so, as it happens, she knew the area but didn't say. Anyway, she said, her evenings were taken up mostly with writing, transcribing her interviews and catching up with an endless backlog of reading and online research. This had the effect of slowing down the pace of conversation a little, but the idea of a daytime visit was still a possibility.

Just over a week later, having freed herself up for the afternoon, Carla shut down her computer and drove inland and up into the hills. It was a long drive and by the time she crossed the Miño she was feeling quite tired. But it wasn't far now and before long she was parking up in a quiet spot on the edge of the little *pueblo* and making her way to the church, where she sat herself down on a rough-hewn granite bench in the shade and checked her phone. She knew it was getting a little late for lunch, but Paulo joined her just minutes later, clutching a newspaper and a brown wrapper containing a long loaf of crusty bread. This was something you just *did*, whether you needed it or not.

When she saw him her heart fluttered. She knew exactly what was going to happen and tingled inwardly with a ripple of excitement on seeing him again: a light lunch, plus wine of course (the Ribeiro was very good, he told her); the mandatory tour of the house and the grounds; a siesta… love-making… but she mustn't stay the night. She really must not, she had reminded him. She had to set off early in the morning for an appointment and although he looked a little dented, he seemed to understand.

They kissed sweetly and Paulo showed her briefly around the village. It was small, very traditional and rural, and with no especially large buildings, apart from the church of course. Most of the houses were built from granite and were very old, having been patched up and added to many times. Several more were long-derelict and overgrown, more landscape by now than architecture.

Fortunately, Paulo had arranged a place for lunch in advance and, although it was simple, it was delightful; no frills or unnecessary embellishments, just a near-perfect tortilla, some anchovies on the side, some calamare and, of course, salad and local crusty bread, still slightly warm. It was way too much for her but Paulo had a very healthy appetite, and the wine more than lived up to her expectations. As the conversation flowed so did the wine. Another bottle was ordered and, as Carla relaxed in his company, she forgot all about the time and then realised that she had drunk far more than she had intended to and was now beginning to feel quite tipsy.

When Paulo excused himself, she took a glance at his newspaper. There was a great deal of alarm about yet another wolf attack, the third in a short space of time, with two goats lost and now a young donkey badly injured. And now there were reports of teams of testosterone-fuelled locals roaming the hills with guns in search of the culprit. Carla knew very well that any wolves that remained in this region kept themselves well inland, up in the mountains where they could live undisturbed and disturb no-one in turn.

Returning to the table Paulo saw her finishing the article and skimmed through it quickly himself, with an odd and uneasy interest.

'Does this happen very often?' Carla asked. She was sure he hadn't mentioned anything about having livestock of his own.

'No, this is rare,' he commented. 'This will be a lone wolf, probably one that has been rejected by the pack. Or it might be sick. They are not usually a danger to people... unless it has *la rabia* of course.'

He folded up the paper and gestured to Manolo, the owner, that they were ready to leave. Having enjoyed their long, slow lunch, and both having drunk far too much, they decided it was best to leave the car in the village. So the pair walked slowly up the hill, a long winding kilometre, to his house, and as they walked, and with Carla feeling distinctly heady, she drew herself close into him and hugged his arm. She was instantly struck by just how strong he was.

The house was much as he had described it; very traditional with its thick granite walls and a granite staircase leading up the outside to the original entrance on the first floor. At ground level there was an extensive and dark *cuadras*, where the animals would originally have been housed, and this still had quite a bit of work to do on it and contained all of Paulo's tools and building materials; people didn't steal things around here. Upstairs, though, was habitable, even comfortable, and was being very tastefully restored, retaining most of its best traditional features including the original chestnut beams. One corner, she noticed, was covered by a large rectangular board which was his ladder access to the *cuadras* below. Soon this would be the staircase between the two floors. Upstairs was a double bedroom and a small spare room overlooking the fields to the west. The grounds, too, were lovely, though still overgrown and untended-to, with plenty of space and not at all overlooked. One day it could be really beautiful.

After exploring the house and the land and the surrounding area for a while, conversation began to waver a little. Both were tired and a little the worse for wear and, with an exchange of looks, they headed quietly back, hand in hand, and upstairs to bed.

Carla found their lovemaking truly wonderful. Paulo was so strong and powerful, yet at the same time so tender and gentle, that she felt almost like a child in his arms until, exhausted and happy, she fell fast asleep with her head on his chest whilst stroking his strong arms with her fingertips.

She hadn't meant to sleep for so long. The sun was already starting to go down behind the hills when she finally woke, though Paulo was still fast asleep beside her.

She had to go. Trying her best not to wake him she gathered up her things and carried them out of the room with her, where she quickly pulled them on and tip-toed her way downstairs. She would call him as soon as she got home and apologise profusely. There was no time to waste.

In a panic, she was already running when she reached the road and she continued down the hill as fast as she could until she reached her car with a huge wave of relief, just as the moon was beginning to rise over the hills. But even as she reached into her bag for her keys she remembered, feeling sick in the pit of her stomach, that they were not there. She remembered distinctly now putting them in her jacket pocket...and then, stupidly, she had left her jacket behind at the cafe-bar.

'Stupid! Stupid! *Stupid!*'

She dared not go back to collect it. Already the backs of her hands were starting to become covered with hair, her nails were toughening and lengthening into claws, and she could feel her face elongating with that strange and powerful animal yearning that overtook her each time this happened. Once more she became acutely aware of her surroundings: the sounds of a car in the distance and of people, not so far away; the dizzying smells of the all the different animals that had passed this way... and especially those of humans. The hair on the back of her shoulders bristled involuntarily at this.

Unable to get away, she glanced about her quickly and, pulling herself up to full height, let go a low, mournful howl before dodging quickly into nearby woodland and heading off in a long wide arc back up the hill from where she came.

21

The Royal Road

Phillip was on a train. What was he doing here? He never travelled by train. He hated trains. Looking out of the carriage window, he could see it was late evening and the light was fading as the strange scenery whizzed by in a confusing blur. There was a long tunnel up ahead as well; he just knew it, and something about it frightened him out of his wits. So he turned to his crossword.

4 Down: five letters:

Phillip had seen this one before, he was sure of it; Franco German agreement goes by the board. *Franco German agreement? Goes by the board?*

He tapped his teeth with his pen.

Agreement! Of course! OUI... JA... Ouija! Ouija BOARD! He carefully penned in the letters in neat black capitals and then looked for adjacent clues. He now had a letter 'I' in 8 Across.

The word, *RECKONING* kept on going round and round in his head. Well, it did have an 'I' but the answer he wanted had twelve letters.

'*RECKONING,*' the little voice repeated.

'But it's only nine letters!' Phillip protested, loudly this time, and the sound of his own voice took him oddly by surprise.

8 Across: twelve letters in all; four, two, three, three. And the fifth letter was an 'I'. Definitely not 'RECKONING!'

'*RECKONING,*' said the voice in his head once more.

People were staring at him.

'You've always got your nose buried in the bloody paper,' Theresa suddenly complained out of nowhere.

Someone a few seats behind her cheered and a tall man at the far end of the carriage started playing the banjo.

Phillip tried to ignore them but his concentration was broken so he closed his paper for the moment and turned his attention to the front-page news.

'Covid Outbreak Out of Control; Millions Feared Dead,' ran the headlines.

'Millions feared dead…' he mused.

Quickly he pulled his mask up over his nose and carried on reading.

This was dreadful news!

Theresa now had her arms wrapped around the neck of the banjo player while he carried on playing his slow, monotonous tune:

Beep… Beep… Beep… Beep…

On the seat, next to Phillip, there was a large blue holdall containing a vast amount of stuff, including dozens of bags of wine gums, a ginger cat, and a thick cable-knit maroon sweater. It was July, and broad daylight all of a sudden! The carriage was roasting hot and now he regretted bringing it, even to Scotland! Anyway, it was completely covered in cat-hair by now.

Theresa called him again, this time on his mobile, with yet another of her angry diatribes. He tried to shut her off but she started singing loudly from the front of the train and the banjo-player joined in. Now everyone was staring at him and singing along in a mocking chorus:

'Ring-a-ring o' roses, a pocket full of posies.'

Phillip switched off his phone but he could still hear them all just as clearly in the background:

'A-tishoo! A-tishoo!'

He was getting angry now. Why wouldn't she just let him be? Why did she have to plague his life like this?

'Plague... Ring o' roses... Of course!'

Phillip reached into his holdall for his book and now it lay unopened next to his crossword puzzle.

SLOW TRAIN TO NOWHERE, read the title, by Denis Hettish. Except he'd never heard of Denis Hettish before and had no idea why he had his book in his holdall. But the plot sounded vaguely interesting and a quick glance suggested it was reasonably well-written.

It was a big book, oddly heavy – and dusty – and opening it randomly at page 39 he read:

Theresa and Paul lay blissfully in each other's arms as the sun slipped slowly beneath the horizon.

'What the hell is this!' he blurted out, even louder this time.

Everyone in the carriage was staring at him and Theresa, now wearing a ridiculous hat, was laughing straight at him.

'Who the hell is Denis Hettish! Why is he writing about you?' he shouted.

He flicked through the pages and there she was again, and again… she seemed to be on every single page.

He tried to distract himself and turned back to his crossword but, as he scanned the clues once more, there was the mysterious author again.

8 Across: *What Denis Hettish reportedly said*; twelve letters; four, two, three, three… and the fifth letter was an 'I'.

Phillip's attention was suddenly diverted by the hugely overweight man sitting nearby who now had no trousers or underpants on. He was singing quietly to himself as though nothing was remotely amiss.

'Put your mask on,' a woman opposite him was insisting. 'You'll catch your death.'

The man ignored her and carried on singing to himself.

He looked grotesque.

The woman was shouting now, *'Put your bloody mask on!'*

Suddenly she broke off hostilities and turned to Phillip. Looking him squarely in the face, she started calling softly to him:

'Hello... Hello... Mr. Randall, can you hear me?'

'How does she know my name? Who is she? What's going on here?'

He quickly turned his attention away from her. He didn't want to appear to be staring at a half-naked man so he turned back to his crossword puzzle and printed the name *DENIS HETTISH* in the top margin.

'Beep... Beep... Beep... Beep...' went the banjo player.

Theresa was still laughing at him and the fat man with no trousers on ran down the carriage and hit her squarely in the face.

Suddenly everything went quiet as the train entered a tunnel and the lights went dim. But still Phillip couldn't get Denis Hettish out of his mind. Was he another one of Theresa's sex-obsessed admirers?

'Two letters, beginning with an 'I'. It had to be *it* or *is* –

or *in*, perhaps!' He looked at the neatly printed name again, *DENIS HETTISH*, and counted the letters. 'Twelve letters... *of course!* It's an anagram!'

It had suddenly turned quite chilly and he thought again about that sweater. And the tunnel seemed to be getting darker, though he could still see his crossword and started to toy with a possible answer, printing it out beneath the mysterious author's name:

THIS...IS...THE... ...

'Hello... Mr. Randall, can you hear me?'

It started to get lighter again, almost bright. Someone was holding his hand.

With a sudden start he realised his mistake: it wasn't four, two, three, three, at all, but two, four, three, three. Phillip quickly crossed through what he had written and printed out the words beneath:

IS... THIS... THE... ...

Before he could finish, the light suddenly got very bright and he could make out strange shadowy shapes and figures around him. And that soft voice again:

'Hello... Mr. Randall, are you with us? Can you hear me?'

Beep... Beep... Beep... Beep... went the banjo player.

'Mr. Randall, I'm Sharon, your ICU nurse, can you hear me?'

She was holding his hand. It was warm, comforting and warm… and soft. But it felt a bit odd too, a bit rubbery. And now he could see her looking down into his face but wearing a mask over her nose and mouth and a large, clear plastic visor over her face. The other shapes around him, too, were turning into people. They also had masks on and plastic visors and dark blue uniforms and aprons. It seemed very bright. And his throat and his chest hurt like hell! He winced as he looked up into her eyes.

'Hello… Mr Randall. Are you with us now?' You've had a difficult time.'

About the Author

Vic Blake was born in May 1947 in the London Borough of Fulham, soon after the end of the Second World War.

At the age of twelve his family moved away from London to Hertfordshire where he left school, aged fifteen, with no recognisable qualifications. After holding down a series of unskilled/semi-skilled jobs, he joined the army – as he says, to escape from his difficult father.

Later, having left the army, he drifted for a while before training and settling down as a teacher. He completed his Masters' degree in 1984 but, while doing background research for a PhD, he became seriously injured in a head-on car crash and was left partially disabled and in constant pain.

Nearly a decade later, still troubled by pain and now losing his hearing, he took early retirement from teaching and began a three-year course in counselling and psychotherapy.

Being a committed profeminist, he developed a keen interest in working with men and this was to become a whole new direction in his life.

Still affected by pain, however, he was forced eventually to retire altogether but continued to research and write on men and masculinity issues. More recently he has turned his hand more seriously to writing fiction.

He now lives in Nottingham with his wife Maggie.